Reflections of a Vampire (A Memoir) A Novel

Anna Elizabeth

Copyright © [2024] by [Anna Elizabeth]

All rights reserved.

No portion of this book may be reproduced in any form without written permission from the publisher or author, except as permitted by U.S. copyright law.

Published by: Jo Ann Gray

Reflections of a Vampire (A Memoir) A Novel

By Anna Elizabeth

Contents

Dedication	1
Reflections of a Vampire (A Memoir) A Novel	2
Prologue	3
Chapter 1	15
Chapter 2	30
Chapter 3	44
Fullpage image	59
Chapter 4	60
Chapter 5	73
Chapter 6	90
Fullpage image	103
Chapter 7	104
Chapter 8	120
Chapter 9	135
Fullpage image	146
Chapter 10	147
Chapter 11	159
Poem: Vampire in the Mirror	166

Poem: A Twisted Oak	170
Poem: Reflections in Silver	172
Fullpage image	176
Fullpage image	177
Fullpage image	178
Fullpage image	179
Reflections of a Vampire	180

Dedicated to 'Anna', my 'daughter' that I never knew!
May you fly high in Heaven!

Dedicated to my son, Dustin!
The best son a mother could ever dream of having!

Reflections of a Vampire
(A Memoir) A Novel

Prologue

Looking back. Reflections of one's life. The pain, the sadness, only moments of bitter happiness. So, my tale can now be told. I'm Maria Grace, an immortal, a vampire. I've been undead for decades now, even centuries. I've seen a lot, felt a lot, and loved far too much over these saddened years, especially in my mortal days. As I ponder back, I find my memories interwoven with both pain and fleeting joyous moments, though only brief ones. They rise like the mists that hang over the bayou at dawn. Beautiful, yet thick with the weight of sorrow. I have wandered through the shadows of this world witnessing the ebb and flow of humanity as the years unfurl like the petals of a wilting flower.

This tale, this story, is not for the faint of heart. This history, I'd like to share, consists of my mortal life leading up to my immortal life.

It is a history steeped in darkness, with secrets untold, now revealed. The past, the present, a life of regrets, and bitter, hard choices made. A vampire's memoir, if you will, woven through the threads of my mortal life leading to the cursed immortality that now binds me. Reflections of an undead being stepping back into the past, into a world of regrets and bitter moments of happiness.

At the age of twenty-seven, I was changed forever, but I would like to start from the beginning...

As a child I was fragile, sickly, a delicate wisp of a girl trapped in a body that betrayed me. By the age of five I was deathly ill. My skin was as pale as the moonlight, my spirit wavering like a candle in the wind. My parents seemed to have given up on any hope of my survival. Once filled with hope, they seemed to have surrendered to despair. I was diagnosed with a rare blood disease, which was basically cancer of the blood in today's language, but in my childhood days it was unheard of to have such an illness, an unspeakable affliction. The only doctor, physician, was the local physician in the small town of New Orleans. This strange gray-haired man was short, almost gnome-like, and spoke with a growling voice, sending shivers down my spine. He frightened me a little. He would try his best to treat my illness, but despite his frantic efforts, he hadn't any idea what was harming my body. The blood transfusions were extremely painful, but the doctor swore it was needed. As this scary, short man would wipe the sweat from his forehead, I would always get nervous. My pain was almost unbearable, especially since I was a child and did not understand why this doctor was hurting me. It seemed he was ill-equipped to handle my type of illness. As he tried to drain the poison from my veins, my mother would cry as she held my hand while the doctor drained the harmful blood from my body. The doctor's sweat poured down his forehead, a reminder of the battle he waged against an enemy he could not see or understand. Each time the needle pierced my fragile skin, I felt a little piece of my childhood slip away.

Then, one fateful night, everything changed. A woman named Melissa stepped into my life, a figure cloaked in shadow and mystery. I thought I was only dreaming, but her beauty was haunting, and I felt an inexplicable pull toward her. She was unlike anyone I had ever seen, with dark, lengthy hair and eyes like emeralds. It seemed her eyes sparkled in the dim moonlight. I was frightened beyond belief as I wondered where she came from and how she entered my room. My mother was fast asleep beside me while I was frozen with fear, and tears of silence creeping down my cheeks as I squeezed my blanket tighter under my chin.

Though I did not know it at the time, she was a vampire, an immortal being who would alter my destiny forever. With her blood, only a few drops to my lips, she healed me, pulling me back from the precipice of death. Yet, there was a small price to pay for this healing. My mother, in a moment of unearthly compassion became her sacrifice. I watched in horror as Melissa drained the life, the blood, from my mother, a ritual that twisted the bond of love into something grotesque. My father was long forgotten since he left us months ago, so no one was there to defend us from this scary being of a lady.

Alone in the world, I was taken in by Melissa, who raised me in the dim, shadowy corridors of a brothel, within the French Quarter. I had forgotten all about that horrid night when Melissa murdered my mother. I was so young and naive, thinking Melissa was my Saviour, my keeper. The brothel house became my new home.

The years slipped by, and at the age of twenty, I found a flicker of happiness in the form of Patrick, a frequent visitor to the brothel. Our connection was instant, electric, as though our souls recognized one another across the void of existence. He was slightly older than myself, but I did not mind. In those stolen, private moments, I believed in love, in something pure amid the sordid backdrop of my unpredictable life.

But love, as I would harshly learn, is a fragile thing with much pain attached to it. Melissa, with her possessive nature, could not bear to see me with Patrick and the happiness he would bring me. She made him vanish, disposed of him, though I did not realize it at the time. She made him disappear like mist under the morning sun. Despair consumed me, and I was left to wander through the echoing halls of my sorrow, haunted by unanswered questions that seemed to never have any justice. 'Where did he go?' 'Why would he just leave?'

In many attempts to console me, Melissa gifted me with a vintage, silver mirror. It was a small thing, yet it sparkled with an otherworldly light, and she told me it was very special. She would express tales of how this small mirror could even let a vampire, an immortal, see its reflection perfectly. She vowed it was a token of her affection to me. Perhaps, it was affection, love, or just a way of filling the void of guilt. I clutched it to my chest, but it felt heavy, like a stone in my heart.

In that dim, moonlit room of the brothel house within the quiet streets of what is now the French Quarter, I sat holding the small, vintage mirror, tracing the intricate designs with my fingertips, as I thought about Melissa. I thought of how she possibly loved and cared for me, of how she only wanted me to be at peace and to always be safe. Lies, it seems now, that were told to keep me with her.

Days turned into weeks, weeks turned into months, and months into years, as Melissa spun tales of romance and adventure, in hopes of cheering up my spirits. Her stories felt hollow in the absence of my Patrick, yet vaguely they did seem to soothe me as she spoke them to me. I remember one of the tales she had spoken of...

'Once long ago, in a forgotten village, there was a lady who lived in the town's brothel house with her estranged aunt. Her name was Grace. She was a spirited girl with brown eyes and wavy brown hair. She was only seventeen when she became an immortal creature who feeds on men draining them of their blood to survive. It was on a dark, rainy night when a gentleman of stature came into the brothel house. He approached the bar and ordered a whiskey shot. Grace was working behind the bar for the bartender that evening since he was lazy and did not want to do his job. This mysterious man was tall and dark with a faded gray beard. Grace was instantly intrigued. This gentleman connected quite well with Grace, and they became intimately acquainted. By morning, in Grace's bedchamber, she awoke alone, and the mysterious man was gone, never to be seen again. Grace was forever changed. She was now a vampire in the making, with only a human's blood to sustain her from her humanity. As nights passed on, Grace could no longer stand the sunlight, it was torturous on her skin. Her aunt noticed something wasn't quite right with her, but she dared not intervene. One late night, as Grace was in her bedroom, she became unbearable. The hunger for a human's blood overtook her. She could smell the aroma of blood in the air. The urge led her to her aunt's room where she was sleeping soundly. Grace brutally murdered her aunt and drained all the blood from her body, as she felt fearless, satisfied. The legend is, Grace still resides in an old brothel place even now. She can never die. She must survive on blood alone for all eternity.'

These silly tales were told to me very often by Melissa, and they always seemed to end in some kind of tragedy. At the time, I figured she was obsessed with these strange, eerie stories of vampires, but I would soon come to realize that Melissa was speaking about her own experience. The story of Grace, who I imagined to be, actually, Melissa, of how she was sadly turned into an immortal. She loved to relate romantic tragedies to me, and I must admit, I did enjoy our quiet moments late at night as Melissa would tell these tales, while we rested in our bed sipping on some type of alcoholic beverage or dwelled in some quiet room of the brothel house. I shall share several of these tales told to me by Melissa as I write this memoir to you, some much longer than others, yet they still seem to vaguely reflect on Melissa's past. One such tragic, yet romantic tale was...

'In the gritty yet romantic London of the 1500's, tells the sad story of Sara and Dustin, two young souls who find love amidst hardship. Sara, a young woman of delicate health, falls madly in love with Dustin, a struggling poet. Their brief time together is filled with much passion and tenderness, but Sara is struck by a relentless fever. As Dustin fights against a cruel fate to save her, he watches her life slowly slip away. In a city steeped in shadows and great beauty, he finds himself utterly alone, forever marked by the love that changed his life, if only for a fleeting moment. The year was 1546, and the streets of London were shrouded in a damp, chilling mist that clung to the alleys like a persistent ghost. People bustled through the wet streets, heads down, minds on survival, but among them was Sara, a slender figure who moved with an almost ethereal grace. Her laughter was soft, comforting, but infectious, like the chiming of distant bells, a rare sound in a world where joy was a scarce commodity. Sara worked as a seamstress, her delicate fingers weaving beauty from the drab fabrics she was given. Her life was simple and quiet until one evening when she met Dustin. A poet with little to his name but a genuine heart full of longing, Dustin had grown up knowing that love was a thing for fairy tales, but when he saw Sara's warm, soothing smile, something within him came to life. Her kindness, her laugh, her fierce spirit, all of it drew him in like a magnet. They met in the busy market, where Dustin had gone to sell his poetry to anyone who would listen. He approached her with a sonnet in his hands, an offering as humble as it was sincere. Sara's cheeks flushed, and her eyes sparkled as she read his words. She was unaccustomed to such attention, especially from someone who looked at her as if she were a blessed miracle. From that day, Sara and Dustin met whenever they could, their time together stolen from the demands of their lives. They walked the water's banks, their laughter mingling with the murmur of the river. Dustin would recite his poems to her, his words full of the yearning he could never quite put into prose, and for Sara, those moments with him felt like breathing pure air after a lifetime in darkness. As winter began to settle over London, Sara and Dustin's love grew much stronger, much closer. They would meet in private, hidden corners, under the arches of crumbling buildings, whispering secrets and inner dreams, their deepest desires to one another as if there were no world beyond the two of them. London's hazy, grayness could not touch them; they had created their own warmth, a sanctuary away from the bleakness of the bust streets. One evening, as they walked near the Tower Bridge, Sara began to cough, a small, innocent sound that Dustin might have dismissed had it not returned the following days, each time more insistent, more painful to Sara. Her skin grew pale, her eyes fever-bright, but she brushed it off with a small chuckle, saying, "It's only the winter chill. Pay it no mind, my love."

But Dustin couldn't just ignore it, the deepening shadows under Sara eyes, the way she trembled as if every breath were a struggle. He began to stay close to her, his poet's heart aching at the thought that something so beautiful could be in such pain. He would hold her as she shivered, his arms wrapped around her tightly, as if he could shield her from whatever illness, whatever sickness, whatever fever was tightening its grip on her frail body. Days passed, and Sara's condition worsened. She was now plagued by a deeper fever, her skin hot to the touch, her once-bright laughter reduced to weak smiles. Dustin, unable to bear the thought of losing her, sought every remedy he could find, visiting apothecaries and divine healers across the city. He would sit by her bedside. pressing cool cloths to her fragile brows, whispering poetry in the hopes that his words might reach some part of her that the fever had not yet taken. "You're going to get better, my sweet Sara," Dustin would promise her, his voice unsure, breaking, "You must. I cannot live without you."

But Sara, with a look of quiet resignation, would only smile a faint, fragile smile, a weakly gesture, as if she already knew a truth he refused to see. The night Sara's fever reached its peak was one that Dustin would remember with painful clarity for the rest of his life. The wind howled outside, rattling the shutters of her small room, while inside, Sara lay beneath the wool blankets, her breaths shallow and uneven. Dustin sat beside her, clutching her hand as if his very life depended on it. Sara turned to him; her eyes unfocused yet still filled with the love that had bound them together. "Dustin," she whispered, her voice no more than a fragile breath, "I dreamed of you last night. We were... by the sea. The sun was shining brightly, and we were free as the birds that fly high in the sky... oh, how I wish..." Her words dissolved into a cough, one that wracked her body and left her gasping for air. Dustin's heart twisted with fear, every instinct within him screaming to do something, to fight against the inevitability that seemed to hover over them like a dark shadow. "Sara, please... don't leave me," he begged, his voice choked with much emotion and feelings. "You're all I have. Don't let the fever take you from me."

A warm tear slipped down Sara's cheek as she reached up, her fingers frail and trembling as she touched his saddened face, "My love," she murmured, her words filled with a heartbreaking tenderness, "You have given me a happiness that I never dreamed possible. If I must go, then let it be with the memory of you being so close to my heart."

Dustin did not want to accept her words, he couldn't bear to let her go. He held her in his arms as close as he could, his own mournful tears falling down his face as he whispered promises, swearing to love her beyond time, for all eternity, beyond life itself. The night stretched on, and Dustin remained by her side, clinging to the faint hope that dawn would bring a miracle, but as the first light of the morning crept into the room, Sara's breathing slowed, her hand slipping from his grasp. The fever, relentless and merciless, had finally claimed her life. The world was seemingly an empty, colorless place without Sara. Dustin wandered through the streets of London as a hollow shell, his mind consumed by the image of her still face, her gentle smile frozen in eternal peace. The love that had once filled his heart now felt like a knife, cutting him with every step he took. His poetry, once filled with the warmth of Sara's love, now turned dark, full of despair and deep longing. He wrote verses for Sara, each word soaked in sorrow, hoping that somehow, some way, his words might reach her wherever she was. Dustin spent his nights by the river where they had once walked, his voice echoing in the emptiness as he recited his poems to the indifferent water's banks, each line a lament for the love he had too soon lost. In the weeks that followed Sara's passing, Dustin tried to find solace in the places they had once shared. He would sit by the fire, his hands clutching the scraps of poetry she had read, her favorite lines marked by the faintest smudges from her fingertips. Every piece of her he held onto felt like a lifeline, and yet, they were mere shadows of the woman he had truly loved so fiercely. He was haunted by her last words to him, the way she had whispered of the happiness he had given her. It felt like both a blessing and a curse. Dustin was left with memories that warmed his heart, even as they tore him apart, memories that reminded him of the life he had lost and the only love that he could never reclaim. Unable to face the reality of a world without Sara, Dustin poured his grief, his painful sorrow, into his work, his poetry. He crafted poem after poem, each one a testament to Sara, to the love that had burned so brightly and ended so cruelly. His words became his only comfort, his only means of keeping her spirit alive in a world that had moved on without her.

One evening, as he sat in the dim light of his room, Dustin began to write his final ode to Sara, a piece that would capture her essence, her beauty, her hypnotizing laughter, all the things he could never forget. His hand trembled as he wrote, each word drawn from the deepest part of his soul, as the heated tears rolled down his cheeks onto the paper. When he finished, he read it aloud, his voice breaking with much emotion as he spoke the final lines...

'Though fever's kiss has claimed thee so,

My heart shall burn wherever I go,

For love, though brief, like fleeting breath,

Shall conquer all, even the coldest death.'

As he quoted those final words, Dustin felt a strange sense of peace, a quiet resignation. Sara might be gone, but his love for her would live on, immortalized in the verses he had just written. Though she would never return to him, he had captured a part of her that no sickness, no death, could ever erase. Dustin folded the poem and set it beside her faded, black and white picture, knowing that he had given her all he could. His heart ached, but for the first time since she had left him, he felt as though he could breathe. Sara had been his muse all along, his true love, his best friend, and though she was now gone, the words of his poem, he had just written in her memory, would remain, a tribute to a love that, while tragically short, had changed him forever.

The fragile, beautiful romance between Sara and Dustin, set against the shadowed streets of London in the 1500's expressed their love, though brief, it became a powerful force, transcending the pain of loss. Dustin's poetry still stands as a timeless monument to their undying love, even as it leaves him haunted by the memory of a fragile life that he could not hold on to, that he could not keep.'

Melissa's tales, though sad at times, always thrilled me, always striking my heart, yet I always wondered why she would say such tragic stories.

One dreary night, Melissa finally revealed the truth, although, she did not admit she was a vampire, an actual immortal being. She confessed to taking my mother's life the night she healed me with her blood. This revelation shattered me. She had given me her sacred blood to sustain my life, my existence. She admitted to disposing of my only love, Patrick. She claimed she needed me to always be with her, never to leave or flee from her. Fury coursed through my veins like fire, igniting a rage I had never known. I lost all control of my emotions, driven by a primal urge for pure vengeance. I confronted Melissa, and in that fateful clash, I became a killer. Her blood, her undead life, stained on my hands, a mere mark of my fatal transformation. As I drove the rusty dagger, from the vanity table, deep into her unbeaten heart, she buried her fangs into my neck in defense. With force, she attacked me while the dirty knife still resided in her chest. As she brutally sucked the blood from my body, I pushed against her chest in hopes of being released from her grasp. Feeling weak and drained, I gave up trying to be free of her. Placing my blood-stained hands over my mouth, I cried out in pain as I thought my life was ending. Melissa was so strong and fierce against my body, yet she was dying. I could fill her going limp as she toppled to the wooden floor. Her lifeless body lay quietly on the planks of the floor, yet she was still so beautiful as she appeared to be gazing at the stars in the night's sky with her glassy, emerald eyes. Kneeling next to her, I pulled the dagger from her bloody chest tossing it across the deserted room. That's when I tasted something strange on my lips, it was Melissa's blood. I passed out.

As I look into this vintage mirror that I still possess, I remember Melissa and the sweeter moments we shared. I comb out my long, thin black hair as I shed a small blood tear from my blue eyes. Now, I reside in the very hotel that was once that brothel house, a sanctuary of memories both bitter and sweet, in the heart of the French Quarter in New Orleans. The echoes of my past linger in the air, and as the moon rises, I reflect on the choices that have shaped my immortal existence, but the world of immortality was far from the sanctuary I would've imagined.

This is my story, a tapestry of love, loss, and the unrelenting shadow of regret, and it begins anew with the whispered memories of a girl who once believed in the promise of life, only to become a creature of the night. Although, it is not in any proper order, my tale, but it is the truth I speak of. This is my memoir, my reflections of a vampire...

Chapter 1

As I sit in the dim light of my hotel room, my home, the flickering shadows dance across the walls, like ghosts of the past. I can almost hear Melissa's lilting voice weaving through the air, recounting tales that blurred the line between enchantment and horror. Those moments, both haunting and sweet, linger in my undead mind, offering a bittersweet solace as I reflect on my time growing up in the brothel house.

Melissa was more than a guardian; she was a tempestuous force in my life, both nurturing and fearsome. In the earliest days after my healing, her presence enveloped me like a warm, silken blanket. She would often sit at the foot of my bed; her emerald eyes glinting in the soft light of the oil lamp and tell me little stories that captured my imagination. Each tale was a blend of romance and tragedy, filled with captivating characters who danced across the thin line between love and despair.

"'Once, there was a beautiful lady named Isabella,' she would begin, her voice like velvet, "who lived in a world painted with the colors of dreams. She loved fiercely but was bound by fate, trapped in a love that could never be, her heart was a fragile thing, fluttering like a trapped bird...'"

I would hang on her every word, imagining myself as Isabella, lost in a world of vibrant hues. Melissa had a way of weaving her narratives that made me believe in magic, even amidst the shadows of the brothel house. Those nights felt like stolen treasures, a sanctuary from the grim realities that surround us. Growing up in the brothel house was a strange mixture of innocence and knowing. The air was thick with scents of jasmine and something darker, and the sounds of laughter, flirtatious gestures, and whispered secrets filled the old, wooded hallways. I was a child among women who lived by their own rules, navigating a world that teetered on the edge of the surreal. I learned quickly to keep my head down, to move with grace among the shadows, blending in with the murmur of hushed conversations and the rustle of skirts. Despite the sordid backdrop, there were moments of joy that flickered like candles in the dark. I remember the impromptu dance parties in the parlor of the brothel, where the women would twirl and spin, seductive laughter echoing against the walls, momentarily erasing the weight of their lives. Melissa would often lead these festivities, her laughter ringing out like a bell, vibrant and alive. I would watch in awe, feeling infectious rhythm pulsate through me, imagining I was one of those pretty ladies in their fancy dresses and silk stockings; I felt a part of something greater. Yet, beneath the immense laughter, I sensed a tension in the air. The brothel house was a world of secrets, where glances exchanged held a thousand unspoken words. The women would sometimes huddle together, sharing whispers that made their eyes shine with mischief or darkened with shame and despair. I longed to join them, to understand the depths of their lives, but Melissa would always draw me close, protecting me from the complexities she deemed too heavy for my fragile heart.

"Not all stories end happily, my dear. This kind of life wasn't meant for you, Maria Grace." Melissa would remind me, a hint of sadness through her words. "Life can be cruel, and the shadows often linger longer than the light."

I clung to her words, both intrigued and frightening, yet I did not truly comprehend them at that moment in time. Melissa was a paradox, a figure of light and darkness who captivated me with her tales. Each story served as a reminder of the dangers that lurked just beyond the threshold of our estranged sanctuary, yet I could not help but admire her strength, her ability to navigate a world that often seemed intent on devouring the weak of heart.

As the years passed, the innocence of my childhood began to fade, like the waning light of dusk. My bond with Melissa deepened, yet I felt an undercurrent of unease, a sense that her love came with strings tied tightly around my heart. I wanted to believe she was my protector, my savior, but shadows danced just outside the periphery of my understanding, teasing me with the truth I was not yet ready to face. There were nights when I would lie awake, staring at the blackened ceiling, listening to the sounds of the brothel house, the soft murmur of voices, the distant laughter, and the occasional sigh that echoed through the dark hallways. I would wonder about the women who inhabited this world, their lives woven together by choice or circumstance, and where I fit into their tapestry. They did feel like a family to me, but I still felt a distance in my heart. Melissa would often come to me, sensing my restlessness. She would sit beside me, brushing my ravenous hair back from my forehead, her touch both tender and possessive.

"You are special, Maria Grace," she would whisper, her eyes gleaming with an intensity that both comforted and frightened me. " Never forget that you are truly loved, the world outside may be dark, but I will always protect you."

In those moments, I wanted, so badly, to believe her, to trust her, trust in her safety and the promise of her words, but as I grew older, the shadows seemed to deepen. The weight of her love began to feel like a chain, binding me to her, even as I yearned for some type of freedom. I watched as she navigated her duality, a caregiver and a predator, leaving me to question the very nature of our estranged bond. Yet, even now, as I reflect back on those times, I can't help but remember the good, the laughter, the stories, and the fleeting moments of joy that Melissa had gifted me with all those years. They shimmer like stars in the night sky, illuminating the darkness that looms ever closer. Each memory is a bitter reminder of what once was, a delicate dance between love and sorrow that continues to shape my immortal existence. My thoughts reflect back on a tale Melissa once told me...

Melissa stood by the window, her slender fingers tracing the outline of the fog-covered glass. The moon was high, casting an eerie glow across the landscape outside. A crooked silhouette of an old oak tree loomed in the distance, its branches twisted and gnarled as though frozen in the throes of some ancient torment. I sat across from her, twirling a strand of my dark hair in my fingers, my eyes flicking from Melissa to the massive oak tree through the window. "You've been staring at that old tree for hours, it seems, Melissa. What is it about that tree that captivates you so?"

Melissa sighed, her voice low and distant, like a whisper carried by the wind through the hollow woods. "That tree," she began, "has a story. A dark one. One that haunts this very land. I never thought much of it myself, until I learned the truth to its true meaning."

I leaned forward, slowly, curiosity pulling me closer to Melissa's words, "What truth?"

"The tale of a man and a woman. Long ago, before the oak tree was twisted so badly and before it was broken down, it stood tall, straight, and proud. It was said to be a symbol of love, for it grew on the land of a couple who were bound by passion but cursed by fate."

Melissa turned away from the window, her face shadowed in the dim candlelight, "His name was Elijah, a man of the forest. He had dark hair, the color of night, and eyes that could see through your soul. He was wild, untamed, and deeply in love with a woman named Anna, a beauty of the village. She had hair as red as the autumn leaves, a contrast to the shadows he carried within. They met in secret beneath the massive oak tree, their love forbidden by Anna's family. She was already promised to another man, a man of wealth and great title, someone her father deemed worthy, but her heart belonged to Elijah. They would steal away under the moon's watch, their hands intertwined, whispering promises of eternity beneath the canopy of this very tree." Melissa's voice grew darker, a hint of sorrow lacing her words, "But fate, as often as it does, had other plans for them. One night, as Anna and Elijah met beneath the oak, they were discovered, caught. Her fiancé, a man of much stature, named Marcus, found them, after following his would be bride. Consumed with rage, he brutally struck Elijah down. The life draining from his eyes as Anna screamed out in anguish, but Marcus did not falter, his fury was far from satisfied. He grabbed Anna by the wrist, dragging her away, but she fought him with all she had, clawing at the earth as he dragged her away, her breaking into shattered fragments of bitter pieces."

My fragile breath caught in my throat, "What happened to her?"

Melissa's eyes seemed distant, far away, like she was in a world all her own, as she spoke, "Anna eventually returned to the oak tree, visiting day after day, mourning for her lost lover. She would sit at the tree's base, her body wasting away as grief consumed her. She prayed to the spirits of the woods, to the ancient powers, for one last chance to be with Elijah, but nothing changed, nothing happened."

A chill seemed to fill the room as Melissa continued her story, her voice soft, yet heavy with deep sorrow in her eyes, "Until one night, when the winds howled, and the sky was torn open by a terrible thunderstorm. Anna was there again, under the old oak tree, beneath its faded leaves as the rain rolled from its branches, weeping. Her cries echoed loudly through the trees around the oak. She called and pleaded for Elijah, begging for him to come back to her, and in that moment, a horrible force of nature answered her cries."

Melissa paused, her gaze fixed on the old oak, as she peered back through the window, "The oak tree... it twisted. Its branches curled and groaned, eerily, as if it were alive, as if it were in pain. And then, from the wet earth beneath it, a hand reached up from the soil, a hand blackened and twisted like the roots of the old oak tree, it was Elijah's gruesome hand."

I quietly gasped, "He came back?"

"Not as he was," Melissa replied, her voice now barely a whisper, "He was something else, something much darker and unnatural. His mere body had become part of the old oak, his soul forever bound to it. Anna overcome with great fear, terror, yet she had much joy as she ran to him, as he crawled from the moistened dirt. She embraced his crooked frame, but the moment their skin touched, she too began to change. The curse spread through her, turning her into something more like him, his undead corpse. They became a part of the tree. It consumed them instantly."

Melissa's eyes gleamed with the weight of the tale as she looked at me, "In her final breath, Anna whispered that she would never leave him again, she wanted to be bound to him forever, no matter the cost. And so, the tree took them both, twisting them into its gnarled branches, their souls disappearing, forever intertwined in a tragic embrace within the twisted oak tree."

I shivered, my eyes darting to the dark shape figure of the twisted oak outside the window, "So, they are still in there?"

Melissa nodded, slowly, "Yes. Some say you can hear them on quiet nights when the wind quietly howls, Anna's soft cries of mercy, and Elijah's mournful whispers. Others say the oak tree watches those who walk beneath it, hungry for more souls, more broken hearts, to claim."

A heavy silence settled between us, the weight of the story pressing down like the thick fog outside.

"Why tell me this, this sad tale?" I asked, as my voice trembled with emotion.

Melissa's gaze met mine, something unreadable in her eyes, "Because the twisted oak tree... it calls to those who know its story. It is not just a false tale, Maria Grace. The oak is still very much alive, waiting in silence for the next victim, the next heartbroken soul to wander too close."

For a moment, neither of us spoke, the only sound was the soft rustle of wind outside the window, weaving through the twisted branches of the ancient oak, carrying with it the faint echoes of the past, of a love lost, and a curse that had yet to be discovered. Then, Melissa, breaking the dead silence of the room, quoted a poem...

A Twisted Oak

Beneath the moon's cold, silver stare,

A twisted Oak stands, roots laid bare,

Its branches reach like fingers torn,

From earth's deep womb, dark secrets born,
Its bark is black, like sins confessed,
A graveyard's breath upon its crest,
Once proud, once tall, now bent and scarred,
A witness to two hearts, love-marred,
They met beneath its shadowed veil,
A tale of love, now sharp as nails,
His eyes like night, her hair like flame,
But fate's cruel hand would play its game,
Beneath this tree, where whispers bleed,
They swore their love, and hearts would heed,
But blood was spilt, and vows were torn,
Their love turned ghost, forever mourned,
Now twisted wood and hollow cries,
Mingle with the midnight skies,
A tree of sorrow, dark and grim,
Where lovers' souls twist limb to limb,
So if you pass, be sure to flee,
From the shadow of the oak tree,
For it still hungers, still it waits,
To bind another to its fate.

As Melissa said that last word of this poem, she made her leave, as I dwelled in amazement at the tale I just endured.

In the shadow of this memory, I found solace and despair, forever entwined in the fabric of my past. The brothel, Melissa, and the old, twisted oak tree, once a haven of laughter and tears, now stands as a testament to the complexities of love, loss, and the choices that ultimately led me down the path of darkness.

A story Melissa shared with me one late evening, comes to my mind, though it's a lengthy tale, yet it has significant meaning. Sometimes, Melissa would tell me tales from places I'd never been or seen, faraway places, far from New Orleans...

'The year was 1534, and the land was rife with whispers pf political alliances and family dynasties, where every choice carried the weight of generations. Amidst this chaos, in the rolling hills of Tuscany, two young souls found each other. Luciana, the daughter of a noble family, and Alessandro, the son of a wealthy merchant, crossed paths under the most serendipitous of circumstances. Luciana was of noble blood, her father the powerful Count Ludovico, whose wealth and influence spanned far beyond the borders of their estate. Alessandro, though prosperous in his own right, was not of noble lineage, and thus their love was, from the very start, destined to be fraught with peril. Their first meeting was on the banks of the Arno River, where Luciana often walked to escape the suffocating expectations of her father. The golden light of the setting sun reflected off the river, and it was there that their eyes met, Alessandro, rugged yet refined, with deep brown eyes full of intensity and intelligence, and Luciana, with her hair the color of chestnuts and a smile that could soften the hardest of hearts. It was not long before they found themselves drawn to one another, unable to resist the pull of a love that felt both inevitable and forbidden. For months, they met in secret, stealing moments beneath the shadow of the forest, whispering promises of undying love. Luciana's laughter filled Alessandro's heart, and in her, he found a kindred spirit who understood his dreams and inner ambitions, who saw him as more than a merchant's son. And to Luciana, Alessandro represented freedom, freedom from the expectations of a noblewoman's life, freedom to love without condition or restraint. Yet their love was always shadowed by the knowledge of what loomed ahead. Luciana had been promised to another man, Lord Pietro, a match arranged for mere political gain. Lord Pietro was a man of great wealth and much influence, but he was cold, calculating, and much older than Luciana. It was a union that would secure her family's status, and one her father, Count Ludovico, was determined to see through. Luciana's love for Alessandro, though fierce, was at constant war with the obligation she felt to her family. One fateful evening, while Luciana and Alessandro lay beneath the stars in a meadow far from prying eyes, she spoke of the impending doom that was her wedding to Lord Pietro, "My heart is yours, Alessandro," she whispered, her voice trembling, "but my father... he will never allow this. He sees nothing but titles and lands. What will we do?"

Alessandro's jaw tightened, his hands gripping hers more tightly, "We will run away, Luciana. We will go far from here, to a place where your father's name means nothing. I will provide for us; we will be free, happy together."

But Luciana's eyes filled with warm tears, "There is no escaping my father. He would, most definitely, hunt us down, and his wrath would be swift, and what of my family? I cannot bring ruin to them."

A painful silence fell between them, both knowing that their love was bound by unseen chains they could not break. Yet even as despair gripped their hearts, their resolve only grew stronger. They would, with determination, find a way, or die trying. Count Ludovico was a man who prided himself on his iron will. He was a towering figure, with sharp features and a gaze that could pierce through any man's soul. To him, Luciana was not just his daughter; she was the key to solidifying his family's legacy. Her marriage to Lord Pietro had been arranged since she was a young child, and as the wedding day approached, Count Ludovico grew more impatient with her resistance. He had begun to notice a change in her, his daughter, a distance, a quiet rebellion, though Luciana was careful, the servants whispered of her mysterious absences and secretive demeanor. It wasn't long before the rumors reached Count Ludovico's ears: his daughter was in love with a man of lower station. The very thought enraged him. Luciana's defiance was not merely a slight to him but an affront to the honor of his noble name. Count Ludovico summoned Luciana to his chambers one evening. She entered with her head held high, though her heart pounded in her chest. The walls of his study were adorned with tapestries of their family's long history of nobility, and the air was thick with the smell of burning wood from the fireplace. "My daughter," Count Ludovico began, his voice calm but laced with menace. "I have heard troubling rumors. Rumors that you are consorting with a man unworthy of you, a commoner."

Luciana stood her ground, though her hands trembled at her sides, "Father, I..."

"You will not speak," Count Ludovico interrupted, his voice rising, "You have brought much shame to this family with your foolishness. Do you understand what is at stake? Your marriage to Lord Pietro is not a choice. It is a duty. You will fulfill that duty, or I swear, you will regret the day you were ever born."

Tears brimmed Luciana's fragile eyes, but she refused to let them fall down her cheeks in front of her father, "Father, please, I love Alessandro. He is kind, he is honorable..."

"Enough!" Count Ludovico slammed his fist against the table, causing the ink bottle to spill, "Love? You speak of love? Love is a luxury for those who do not have the weight of entire generations upon their shoulders. You will marry Lord Pietro, and you will never see this Alessandro again."

Luciana's voice was barely a whisper as she replied, "I cannot do that."

"You will," Count Ludovico said coldly, "or I will see to it that this Alessandro is dealt with. Permanently."

The threat hung in the air like a dark cloud, and Luciana felt the ground slip from beneath her. She had always feared her father's wrath, but this... this was something far worse than she had imagined. If she did not comply, Alessandro's life would be forfeit. That night, she wrote a letter to Alessandro, her hand shaking as she penned the words. She told him of her father's threat, of the impossible choice she now faced. Her heart broke with every line, but she knew she had to try and protect him, even if it meant sacrificing her own happiness.

Alessandro received Luciana's letter beneath the cloak of night, his heart pounding as he read her words. He could not just accept this; he would not let Count Ludovico take Luciana away from him. Desperation filled him, and he resolved to act. They would run, just as he promised her before, they would flee before the wedding, before Count Ludovico's iron grip could close around them both. Alessandro rode to the Count's estate under the cover of darkness, knowing that it would be their last chance to escape. He secretly sent word to Luciana through a trusted servant, and they agreed to meet in the old chapel on the edge of her father's lands, a place long abandoned and forgotten. As Luciana made her way to the secluded chapel, her heart raced. She had packed only what she could carry, her mother's locket, a few gold coins, and a dagger she kept hidden underneath her cloak. The chapel was cold and damp, the air heavy with the scent of decay. Alessandro was already there, waiting for her, his face pale but determined. "We must go now," he urged, taking her hands, "I have horses waiting. We can be in Siena by morning, and from there, we can sail for the coast."

Luciana hesitated, her fragile eyes filled with both love and fear, "Alessandro, if we do this, there is no turning back. My father will come after us, once he knows I've disappeared. He will never forgive us; he will never forgive me."

"I do not care, Luciana," Alessandro said fiercely, "I would rather die than live without you."

They embraced, intimately, their hearts beating in unison, and for a moment, it seemed as though they might succeed, but as they prepared to leave the chapel, the sound of many horses and shouting filled the air. Luciana's heart froze in her chest as she recognized the voice of her father's men. They had been found. The doors of the abandoned chapel burst open, and Count Ludovico stormed in, flanked by his guards. His face was a mask of fury, his eyes burning with hatred as they fell upon Alessandro. "You dare defy me?" Count Ludovico roared, his hand reaching for the sword at his side, "You think you can just steal my daughter and escape without consequence?"

Luciana stepped between her father and Alessandro, her arms outstretched, "Father, please, I beg you. Let us go. I love him!"

"You love him?" Count Ludovico spat, "Then you will be shamed after his death!"

Before Luciana could react, Count Ludovico drew his sword and advanced on Alessandro. The guards seized Luciana, pulling her back as she screamed for them to stop. Alessandro, unarmed but resolute, stood his ground, knowing this was the moment his fate had always been leading to. In the blink of an eye, the Count's sword plunged through Alessandro's chest. A gasp escaped his lips as he staggered, blood spilling from the wound. He fell to his knees, his eyes locked on Luciana's as the life drained from him. "No!" Luciana's scream echoed through the chapel, her heart shattering into a million pieces as she watched the man she loved die before her. She broke free from the guards and rushed to his side, cradling his head in her lap as the heated tears streamed down her face. "Alessandro," Luciana whispered, her voice filled with much grief, "Please, stay with me, please."

But it was too late, Alessandro's eyes fluttered closed, and with his last breath, he whispered her name. Luciana's world collapsed around her. In that moment, nothing else mattered, her father's ambitions, the arranged marriage, the future that had once stretched before her. All that remained was the unbearable weight of her loss, the loss of her only true love. As she held Alessandro's lifeless body, Luciana made a vow to herself. She would not marry Lord Pietro. She would not live a life without love. That night, in the darkness of the chapel, she took the dagger she had hidden beneath her cloak and plunged it straight into her own heart, joining Alessandro in death, their souls bound together for eternity.

The news of Luciana's and Alessandro's tragic death spread quickly through Tuscany. Count Ludovico, devastated by the loss of his only child, yet more from the loss of his political arrangement, withdrew from public life, shamed, his once great ambition shattered by his own cruel actions. The Count's estate, once a symbol of power and prestige, fell into ruin, a shadow of its former glory. Lord Pietro left the country without a bride, he married another noblewoman, but the union brought him little happiness, hardly any wealth or mature status. He, too, was saddened, haunted, by the tragic tale of Luciana and Alessandro, a story that would be told for many generations to come. In time, the chapel where they had died became a place of pilgrimage for many lovers who sought to honor their memory. The tale became a legend, and the legend of Luciana and Alessandro, the noblewoman and the merchant's son who defied the world for their love, lived on, a reminder that even in the face of impossible odds, love could not be silenced. Their tragic story became a symbol of love's enduring power, even in the face of tragedy. And so, the lover's tale, though marked by great sorrow, was also one of triumph. For in death, they had found the freedom that life had denied them. Their love, unyielding and eternal, would never be forgotten.'

Melissa's words still linger in my mind, the night she told me this story. I can almost hear the sound of her gentle voice, so clearly, as she related it to me. Her romantic tragedies always left me feeling overwhelmed, at a loss of finding any words to say...

Chapter 2

The soft glow of dawn filters through the lace curtains of my hotel room, my home, casting delicate patterns across the floor. As I sit on the edge of my bed, I can't help but be drawn back, as I reflect the memories of Patrick, the way he entered my life like a breath of fresh air, stirring feelings within me, I had long thought buried. Patrick was everything I had dreamed of during my tumultuous childhood, a radiant beacon amidst the shadows of my existence. He stood tall, with sandy-blonde hair that caught the night, and green eyes that sparkled with an energy that felt almost alive. There was a warmth in him that drew me closer, an intoxicating blend of confidence and kindness that ignited something deeper within me. We met one fateful evening in the parlor of the brothel house, I was sitting in a corner, quietly reading a parchment of paper that contained the stories of make-believe fantasies, trying to escape the world around me. Patrick entered with an easy grace, a newcomer among the familiar faces, or at least, a new face to me. His laughter rang out, genuine and bright, and I remember glancing up to find him smiling toward me, a moment that felt like time itself had paused.

From that day forward, we were inseparable. Each stolen moment felt like an eternity, wrapped in the blissful cocoon of our shared laughter and whispered secrets. Patrick often found ways to sneak into my thoughts when I was dwelling alone, yet he would always find a way to surprise me at night, by sneaking into my secluded bedroom. He would tell me stories of his adventures, dreams of traveling the world with me at his side, and how he believed in a promising future filled with amazing possibilities. In his presence, I felt more alive than I ever had, like the sun had finally broken through the dense fog of my past. I was truly in love with Patrick.

In the dim light of the brothel house, Patrick and I would steal away to the small rooftop terrace, where the stars stretched endlessly above us. He would hold my fragile hand, his mere touch warm and grounding, and speak of everything from the mundane to the magical. I would get lost in the sound of his soothing voice. "One day," he promised, his voice a gentle murmur, "we will escape this place. We will find a better world together, Maria Grace. Just you wait and see."

I honestly believed in his words, clinging to that dream like a lifeline. Each moment spent with him was a safe refuge from the complexities of my life with Melissa, but beneath the joy, I sensed an ever-growing tension, one that had a name, Melissa. Though she pretended to support my happiness with Patrick, I could see the storm brewing behind her emerald eyes whenever Patrick entered the room seeking my affection. There was a possessiveness in her gaze, a flicker of something darker that sent shivers down my spine. I couldn't understand it then; all I knew was that every single time Patrick smiled at me with a sparkle in his eyes, a shadow seemed to cross Melissa's face, tightening the space around us. 'Why does she dislike Patrick so much?' I would question silently to myself, every inquiry falling on deaf ears as I tried to navigate the tumult of my emotions swirling within me.

Melissa would, often times, try to change the subject whenever Patrick's name came up, steering our conversation back to tales of darkness or the lessons she believed I needed to learn. 'She's just trying to protect you, Maria Grace.' I would tell myself, ignoring the gnawing doubt that crept into my heart, like a heavy gut feeling. But her disdain felt palpable, heavy in the air like a storm waiting to break. There were nights when I would hear Melissa and Patrick argue in faint, hushed tones. Melissa's voice sharp with veiled threats and Patrick's voice calm, yet firm responses pushing back against her venom. They were arguing over me, each argument chipped away at my fragile heart, leaving me torn between the woman who had saved my life, raised me as her own child, and the man who had shown me love, who had stolen my heart. Our tender moments, of Melissa telling me romantic, tragic tales, seemed to halt, or at least until, after Patrick's disappearance, but I do remember one story she told me before everything happened with Patrick...

'In the heart of medieval England, the year was 1462, the air in the village of Keswick was thick with the scent of damp earth and smoke from the fireplaces of thatched-roof homes. Life moved with the rhythm of the seasons, and the common folk toiled under the rule of the local nobility, their days dictated by duty, their nights filled with prayers for better fortunes. Amidst this humble setting, a tragic romance was born, one filled with love, jealousy, and ultimately, betrayal. Monica, the daughter of a widowed tailor, had grown into a woman of rare beauty, with hair the color of raven's wings and eyes like darkened seas. Her beauty was whispered about in the village, and many men sought her hand, but it was Henry, a young and ambitious nobleman, who laid claim to her. Henry was a man of intense passions, with piercing blue eyes that seemed to see through the very soul of those around him. His family had amassed wealth and influence through shrewd alliances, and he had his sights set on rising further through strategic marriage. For Monica, love was not what brought her to Henry's doorstep. It was necessity. Her family had fallen on hard times since her father's death, and her mother had grown frail with illness. To marry a nobleman like Henry would provide her with safety, security, and the kind of life her family desperately needed. Henry's attentions were flattering at first. He showered her with elegant gifts, silks from the East, golden bracelets, ornate brooches. His voice was honeyed as he would speak of a life together, but his intentions, as Monica soon discovered, were not those of a man seeking a partner; he sought ownership, for Henry believed Monica to be beneath him, a lower class, deserving of whatever he chose to be fit for her. From the moment, he proposed to her, Monica was no longer treated as a woman to be cherished but as a prize won, a prize to be guarded. The engagement ring he placed upon her fragile finger was as much a shackle as it was a symbol of union. "You are now mine, Monica, my dear," Henry had said the night he claimed her as his fiancée, his voice low and possessive, "No other man will touch you, speak to you, or even look at you without my permission."

At first, Monica convinced herself that this possessiveness was borne of deep love. Henry's passion, after all, was intoxicating. He spoke to her with such devotion, and when he held her in his arms, it felt as though he might crush her with the intensity if his embrace. She thought she could grow to love him, that perhaps this was what love was supposed to feel like, overwhelming, consuming. But as the days turned to weeks, Henry's affection grew darker. He became increasingly suspicious of anyone who so much as glanced in her direction. His jealously festered like a wound that would not heal, and soon it was not just strangers who earned his wrath but those closest to her. Henry's jealously became a constant dark shadow over their relationship. He followed Monica's every movement with a watchful eye, questioning her endlessly about where she had been, whom she had spoken to, and what had been said. The village gossip did nothing to help matters. Monica wasn't even allowed to visit her family, her siblings. Many whispered that a woman as beautiful as Monica could not possibly be loyal to just one man, that surely, other suitors must still be vying for her attention, her affection, in secret. There was one man, in particular, who caught Henry's suspicion, James, a friend from Monica's childhood. James had always been kind to Monica, his manner gentle, his smiles warm. Though they had grown up together, and he had never showed her any intention of courting her, Henry's insecurities twisted their friendship into something far more sinister within his mind. One afternoon, while Monica was in the village, James approached her in the market square. His eyes held the same softness they always had, and he smiled as he greeted her. "Monica," James said, his voice full of affection, "It has been too long since we last spoke. How have you been?"

Monica smiled in return, though she could feel the weight of Henry's imagined accusations already building in her chest, "I am well, James. Life has become... complicated, but I am managing."

James frowned, concern etched across his face, "Is everything all right? You do not seem happy?"

Before Monica could answer, she felt a hand grip her arm, hard. She turned to find Henry standing behind her, his expression dark and menacing. "Is this what you do when I am not with you, my dear?" Henry hissed, his grip tightening, "You cavort with other men, smiling and laughing as if you are free to do as you, so please?"

Monica's heart raced with fear, and she tried to pull away, but Henry's hold was unrelenting, "Henry, please," she pleaded, "James is just a friend. There's nothing..."

"A friend?" Henry's eyes blazed with fury. "I will not be made a fool of! You are mine, and I will not tolerate this... this betrayal."

James stepped forward, his expression firm, "My Lord Henry, you are mistaken. I mean no harm. Monica and I are but friends, I've known her since we were children."

But Henry was beyond reason. His jealousy had twisted into something far more dangerous, possessive madness. He released Monica only to grab James by the collar, shoving him back with a force that sent him stumbling. "Stay away from her," Henry growled, his voice filled with venom, "If I ever see you near her again, I will not be so understanding."

Monica watched in horror as James staggered away, his eyes filled with confusion, sadness rather than anger. She wanted to cry out, to defend her long-time friend, but fear had stolen her voice. After the confrontation, things only worsened. Henry's possessiveness transformed into full-blown control. He forbade Monica from leaving their estate without his permission, even the simplest joys, like walking through the village or visiting her frail mother, were taken from her. Henry's once passionate love had now become a cage, and Monica found herself trapped within it. Her beauty seemed to become a curse to her, instead of a joy. When they were alone, Henry's temper was quick to flare. He would berate her for imagined slights, accuse her of infidelity, and demand that she proves her loyalty over and over again. The gifts he had once lavished upon her now felt like chains, reminders of the cruel control he wielded over her secluded life. Monica's world had become suffocating, and yet she felt powerless to escape it. She had been raised to believe that a woman's duty was to always obey their husband, and though they were not yet wed, Henry had already assumed the role of master over her, and yet, amidst the darkness, there was a small glimmer of hope, the love that had grown quietly, secretly, within her, without her even realizing it, was for James, the only man to be so kind to her. Despite Henry's threats, James had not disappeared from Monica's life. He would cautiously leave small notes for her in secret, expressing his concern for her well-being, his regret at not being able to protect her. The little letters became a lifeline, a hope, for Monica, a reminder that there was still someone in the world who cared for her as a person, as a woman of value, not as a possession. Their correspondence was brief and discreet, but with each passing note, Monica's feelings for James deepened. She began to see in him what she had never seen in Henry, kindness, understanding, and a genuine affection that asked for nothing in return. But Monica knew that any affection between them could never be acted upon. To do so would be to invite Henry's wrath, and the consequences could be dire, fatal. Still, the temptation lingered within her, and the thought of what could have been haunted her thoughts, her dreams. As winter settled over Keswick, a bitter chill crept into Monica's soul. She could no longer deny the feelings she had for James, that seemed to develop in a stronger sense as time crept on, though she dared not speak them aloud. But Henry, ever watchful, began to sense that something was amiss. His jealously, already a poisonous force, began to consume him entirely. He watched Monica's every movement, scrutinized her every word, searching for signs of betrayal. It wasn't long before Henry discovered the secret letters. One evening, while Monica was away tending to her ailing mother, the onetime Henry allowed her to be out of his sight, he searched her chambers, his hands shaking with such suspicion. Hidden beneath a loose floorboard, he found them, small, neatly folded notes with a pink ribbon of satin tied around them, each one bearing James's signature. When Monica returned later, that evening, Henry was waiting for her, the letters spread out before him like damning evidence in a court of law. His face was pale with rage, his eyes cold and unforgiving. "How could you, Monica?" Henry spat, his voice trembling with fury. "How could you betray me like this?"

Monica froze, her heart pounding in her chest, "Henry, please, it's not what you think..."

"Not what I think?" he snarled, rising to his feet, "You've been sneaking behind my back, exchanging love letters with another man! Do you think I am a fool, Monica? Do you think I do not see what is happening?"

Warm, saddened tears welled in Monica's eyes. She had known this day would eventually come, had feared it with every fiber of her being, but now that it was here, she could find no words to defend herself.

"I have done nothing wrong," she whispered, though even she could hear the lie in her voice.

"Nothing wrong?" Henry advanced on her, his expression murderous, "You have betrayed me, Monica. You belong to me, and you have given your heart to another." He grabbed her by the wrist, his grip painful, "You will never see him again, or speak to him in anyway," Henry hissed, "Do you hear me? You will always remain mine and mine alone, or by God, I will see to it that neither of you will live to regret it."

Monica recoiled in fear, her mind racing. She had to do something, anything, to protect James, but as she looked into Henry's eyes, she realized that he was beyond any reason. There was only one way this could end. The days that followed were a blur of tension and hidden fear. Henry had confined Monica to their estate, but much stricter rules, watching her every move, never allowing her a moment of privacy, but despite his efforts, Monica managed to send one final message to James, warning him of Henry's discovery and begging him to leave Keswick before it was too late. James, however, could not abandon her, his love for Monica was too great, and he resolved to rescue her from Henry's cruel clutches, no matter the cost. One cold, moonless night, James crept to the estate under the cover of mere darkness, determined to spirit Monica away. But Henry, ever vigilant, had anticipated this. He was waiting for James in the courtyard, sword in hand, his face twisted with much hatred. "So, the coward finally shows himself," Henry sneered as James approached. "You think you can take her from me? You think you can just steal what is mine?"

"Monica is not yet yours to own, sir." James replied, his voice steady despite the fear coursing through him. "She is her own person, her own heartbeat, and she does not love you. She will not marry you, Lord Henry."

Henry's eyes flashed with fury, "She belongs to me!" he roared, lunging at James with his sword.

The two men clashed in a violent struggle, the sound of steel ringing out in the cold night air. Monica, hearing the commotion, rushed from the manor just in time to see the fatal blow. Henry, his rage blinding him, had driven his sword through James's chest. "No!" Monica screamed, running to James as he fell to the dampened ground, blood pouring from his fatal wound. She cradled him in her frail arms, her painful tears falling into his pale face. "Monica," James whispered, his voice weak, fading, "I'm so sorry... I couldn't save you."

Monica's heart shattered as she held him, her sobs echoing through the entire courtyard. James's breath grew shallow, and with one final look at the woman he loved, he was gone. Henry stood over them, his chest heaving, the sword still clutched in his hand, but as he looked at the lifeless body of James, something inside him broke. The realization of what he had done, what his jealousy had driven him to, washed over him like a cold wave. Monica rose to her feet, her eyes filled with a hatred so fierce it made Henry flinch. "You are a monster," she spat, her voice angered with grief, "You have taken everything from me."

Henry reached for her, but she stepped back, her expression one of pure contempt. "You will never have me, you will never touch me again," she said, her voice, firm, steady despite the tears streaming down her face. "I would rather die than be yours." And with that, Monica turned and fled into the night, leaving Henry alone in the courtyard, his heart as cold and empty as the winter wind that howled through the trees.

Monica disappeared from Keswick that same night, and though Henry searched for her, he never found her. Some would say she had gone to a convent, seeking refuge from the world that had betrayed her, while others would whisper that she had taken her own life, unable to bear the weight of her grief. Henry was left with the consequences of his actions, his wealth and power hollow comforts in the face of the love he had destroyed. The village spoke of him in hushed tones, a man consumed by jealousy and mere madness, a man who had claimed love as ownership and lost everything in the process. In the end, Monica and James's love, though brief and tragic, was the only thing that remained pure, a love that could not be controlled or possessed, a love that was stolen by jealousy but never truly extinguished. And as the years passed, their story became a cautionary tale, a reminder of the dangers of possession disguised as passion, and the destruction that jealousy can bring to even the most powerful man.'

This tragic, sad tale lingered for many days in my hidden thoughts, as I pondered on why Melissa would tell me such a story as this…

As the weeks turned into months, the joyful moments with Patrick began to feel overshadowed by Melissa's dark influence. My heart ached with the knowledge that our love was not meant to flourish freely. It was a fragile thing, held captive in the shadows, while Melissa's watchful gaze loomed over us like a specter. Melissa would frequently make comments toward me, comments of how bad Patrick was for me, and I should end this silly relationship. Melissa would say things to me, in passing, of how I belonged to her, and her alone.

One evening, as we sat beneath the stars, Patrick took my hand in his, his grip firm and reassuring, "Maria Grace," he began, his green eyes searching mine, "I can feel the tension from Melissa, she does not want me around, does she?"

I swallowed hard, a lump forming in my throat, "I... she just cares too much about me, that's all, Patrick. She... she wants to protect me, I believe. After all, she's like a mother to me, she raised me under her wing. It's obviously hard for her to just let me go."

"Protect you from what, Maria Grace? From happiness?" Patrick's voice filled with frustration that echoed my own inner turmoil. "You deserve happiness, to be free, to choose your own path. I can't stand it, or even understand the thought of Melissa being the reason you feel trapped."

Tears pricked at the corners of my eyes. I wanted to believe that love could conquer all, that our bond was strong enough to withstand Melissa's darkness, that she seemed to portray lately. But as Patrick spoke these words to me, I felt a sense of inevitability creeping in, like shadows stretching over the light. Days passed, and the atmosphere between the three of us grew increasingly strained. Patrick began to pull away, it seemed, sensing the mounting tension that I could no longer just ignore. Melissa's grip on me seemed to tighten, her mere presence suffocating. I was caught between two worlds, one filled with love and promise, and the other draped in dark shadows and secrets. Patrick would consistently plead for me to marry him and leave this brothel house for good. He made pleadings of how we would disappear and live far away from Melissa's hold, but there was something holding me here with Melissa, like I just couldn't leave her behind.

Then came that horrible night, that shattered everything within me... I had returned to the brothel house after a long day spent with Patrick in the woods under the old oak tree, we had enjoyed a day of much laughter and conversation of our future, while having a picnic. My heart swelled with warmth and dreams of a life we were going to build together, but as I entered, the air felt thick with foreboding. I found Melissa in the parlor, her eyes aflame with a rage I had never witnessed before. She was pacing, her movements quick and restless, and my heart sank as I recognized the storm brewing within her. "You need to stay away from him, Maria Grace," Melissa hissed, the venom in her voice boiling. "He is a distraction, a weakness that will only bring you pain. Love cannot sustain your inner desires, it will only leave you bitter and destroyed, trust me, I know this from experience. You must let this man go!"

"Melissa, please," I pleaded, desperation clawing at my throat, "He does love me, and I love him! Patrick would never desert me or hurt me in any way. Why is this so wrong to you? Why won't you allow me such happiness?"

"Love?' she scoffed, her disturbing laughter bitter, "You think his love could ever save you, Maria Grace? It will only lead you to your ruin. He doesn't understand what you are to me, what I have given you all these years. He only wants to take you away from me!"

I felt the weight of her words crashing down hard upon my heart, each syllable like a dagger, fear creeping in, "Why must you say such things? I would always be here for you, even if I am betrothed to Patrick."

But before Melissa could answer, Patrick appeared in the doorway, overhearing our words, his expression filled with determination and frustration, "I'm not going anywhere, Melissa," he declared, standing tall despite the danger that hung in the air. "I care deeply for Maria Grace, same as you, and I won't let you scare me away from her."

In that moment, everything shifted, the storm unfolded. Melissa's eyes darkened with anger, and the intense tension in the room became unbearable. The argument between Melissa and me halted, it was between Patrick and her now, with words turning into weapons, leaving me feeling powerless, caught in the crossfire of their wills. In an instant, the air crackled with unspoken promises of destruction, as I watched in horror, Melissa fueled with much rage, turned on Patrick, her form a blur of fury. It was a scene that played out like a nightmare, one that would haunt me for all eternity, as she pounded her enraged fists against his chest. Her eyes seemed to burn with red fire as she screamed words of disgrace at Patrick. He fought back with words of strength, gripping her in his embrace. I stood frozen, tears streaming down my warm cheeks, helpless to even try to intervene. As the struggle unfolded, Patrick's pleadings to Melissa echoed in my ears, desperate pleas for mere understanding and mercy, but they fell on deaf ears. And then, silence. The only faint sound was my quiet cries as the room fell still, the weight of despair settling over us like a heavy shroud. I could hardly breath as I rushed to Patrick's side, as he pushed away from Melissa's defeated rage. I cradled myself against his chest, the warmth of his skin soothing my whirlwind of emotions. I realized in that moment the depth of my loss; my destiny was to leave Melissa behind.

"You... you did this!" I choked out, rage and sorrow intertwining in my heart, as I turned to Melissa, fury igniting within me like a wildfire, "Why would you do this? I only want happiness, not this!"

As Melissa dropped to her knees in front of us, with her hands held out in defeat, "Because he is a threat, Maria Grace." she faintly whispered, her voice cold and devoid of remorse, "He would take you from me, I cannot allow this to happen."

Still cradled in Patrick's arms, my world crumbled around me, as I pondered Melissa's words to me in her defeated state. I felt the fragile strands of my mere existence snapping within me, unraveling like threads pulled away from a tapestry. Melissa had tried to destroy the one piece of happiness I dared to hold onto, and in her eyes, I saw a darkness that could never be extinguished. As I stood here, a storm still raging inside me, I knew that my life would never be the same. Patrick was mine, and with him, the last remnants of my childhood, here in the brothel house, slipped away, my childhood innocence lost. I was left with nothing but the echoes of Melissa's words, a haunting reminder of the love that had once burned between us so brightly, now extinguished in the shadows of, what seems to be, betrayal. I was determined, I would leave with Patrick in the morning, to start our life together far away from the brothel house and Melissa. Patrick and I left Melissa to her defeat, as we made our exit. I said my 'good nights' to Patrick as I went to my room for the remainder of the night.

My desires, my plans with Patrick, never became reality, and so, my heart shattered, I was left to navigate a world where love had been twisted into something unrecognizable, a world where Melissa's darkness loomed ever closer, threatening to consume me whole. She was the only comfort I would find in my shattered life. It wasn't long after that dreadful evening, my love, my Patrick never returned, he disappeared from my life completely.

Chapter 3

As I sit in the silence of my hotel room, the memories of my immortal transformation flood back like a tide, relentless and inescapable. It was a moment that irrevocably altered the course of my life, plunging me into a world where shadows danced, and secrets reigned supreme. The day I became a vampire, a creature of the night, marked the beginning of an eternal struggle for identity, power, and understanding.

The night of my change remains etched in my mind, vivid and haunting. After Patrick's tragic demise, disappearance, I was engulfed in a whirlwind of grief and much confusion. I had just taken the life of Melissa, yet the reality of my actions felt surreal. After her remorseful confession of Patrick's disappearance, her immortal secret of being a vampire, and the murdering of my mother the night she took me in,

I lost all control over my rage and emotions. After our confrontation, I had tasted her blood, a bitter elixir that awakened something deep within me, a hunger that clawed at my insides... blood, a hunger for human blood. It was both a curse and a gift, binding me to a legacy I had never chosen. In the days that followed, I found myself wandering the corridors of the brothel house, now mine by a twist of fate, struggling to come to terms with my new existence. I looked into the vintage mirror Melissa had given me, searching for answers in the reflection, I now see, that felt foreign. The girl I once was, had vanished, replaced by an immortal haunted by the ghosts of her past, a girl I once knew, now forever gone, only a faint memory of her remains.

Learning to adjust to my new life was an arduous journey. I had to teach myself the ways of survival, as the creature I'd become, how to drink blood without succumbing to the primal urge to merely kill, how to move through the night with grace and stealth. Melissa had made it all seem easy, as she kept her secret hidden from me for so long. I recall the first time I fed, the rush of power mingled with the fear of losing control, it was a delicate dance between life and death, a line I had to tread carefully. My human emotions still lingered within me, and I was afraid to take one's life, each encounter, thereafter, was a lesson in restraint. I would seek out those lost souls who wandered too close to the brothel house, drawn in by the promise of warmth and comfort for their inner desires, not realizing the darkness that awaited them. I learned to mask my intentions behind a facade of charm, to lure them in with whispered promises of seduction and soft, playful laughter, and yet, every time I sank my fangs into tender flesh, I felt a pang of guilt, an echo of the love I lost. Of course, these emotional guilts did not linger too long, once the fresh, warm blood fell upon my tongue.

Melissa's ghostly presence still lingered in the faint shadows of the brothel house, a ghost of a memory that taunted me. I would often catch glimpses of her, shrouded in the darkness of the hallways. Some images of her portrayed her feeding on unsuspecting victims that she had taken during her existence, then they'd fade away, as if, they were never there. These sightings always made me jump in fear. I never truly understood what she was doing, or how she had done such things, but I was too naive to comprehend the gravity of all her actions back then. Late at night on most nights, I would actually hear the muffled gasps and moans of her victims, yet I did not realize it then, but she was actually feeding on human beings. My immature mind assumed her to be indulging in her pleasures of the flesh. Often, I caught the scent of blood filling the night air, yet I never understood the smell, until now. I still catch a scent of blood lingering within the halls of the brothel house, after catching a glimpse of Melissa's ghostly figure with her victim.

I reflect back on a night when I overheard Melissa in the privacy of her room, curiosity struck me as I peered through the cracked, wooden door of a dimly, candlelit room. I could hear the faint moaning of a man, and seductive whispers coming from Melissa. My heart pounded in my chest, as I gazed upon the mystical sight of Melissa, as she mesmerized this man like a predator about to claim its prey. I witnessed her forcing this man onto the fragile iron bed, as she draped herself on top of him burying her face into his neck, he moaned even louder. That was my cue to leave, I hurriedly scurried back to my room, closing the door. I felt blushed, yet I was emotionally stirred within myself, what I thought was happening, back then, was not the truth, it was merely Melissa taking her victim's blood.

But my admiration for Melissa was complicated, intertwined with fear and longing to be like her. I craved her approval, yet I could not shake the unease that always settled in my bones. She would very often recite tales to me of immortal beings, weaving stories filled with love, loss, eternal longing, usually ending in some form of a tragedy. I realize now that these stories, these mesmerizing tragic tales, were not just for entertainment; they were lessons cloaked in the shadows of her past. A past that I will never come to know, now that she's no longer. She wanted me to understand the weight of her existence as a vampire, yet I did not know she was one at the time, she wanted me to understand the price of her immortality, even if I had yet to grasp the full meaning behind her tales. I feel saddened, at times, when I think of Melissa, and what her past could've been, a past that made her fear being loved and what exactly made her so bitter toward love.

As the decades rolled by, I learned to wield the power of my new life, my undead existence, taking ownership so many years ago of the brothel house that had once belonged to Melissa. I transformed it into something new, a sanctuary for those seeking refuge in the heart of the French Quarter of New Orleans. I infused the place with a sense of life and warmth, even as I remained a creature of the night, lurking in the shadows. It became a hotel, a haven for travelers and dreamers, a facade of normalcy covering the darker truths of the past hidden beneath the surface. Every room held stories of its own, each guest, a fleeting moment of connection in a world that often felt isolating. I reveled in the laughter that echoed through the halls, yet I could not escape the haunting memory of what had once transpired within these walls. I often stood at the window, gazing out at the streets below, feeling the weight of history resting heavily on my shoulders. I had inherited not just a building, but a legacy of pain, sorrow, brief moments of joy, and an eternity of memories. I often gaze at the very spot where the old oak tree stood, twisted and mysterious, although it's gone now, its memory will forever be in my mind. It was the last place, the last joyful memory, I shared with Patrick.

The strange habits of Melissa often linger in my thoughts, woven into the fabric of my memories. There were nights when she would retreat into her own world, her emerald eyes distant and filled with an unfathomable sadness. She would sit in the parlor, lost in thought, and I would watch her, a mixture of concern and confusion coursing through me. 'What haunted her so? What secrets were behind those emerald eyes? What tragedies did she carry in secret?'

I often catch myself longing for the bond we once shared, the laughter and the stories she would tell me, the painted rays of hope in my childhood within the brothel house. Yet, as I grew older, I began to see the shadows of her darkness, the sadness in her tales, and the darker undercurrents that hinted at a life steeped in much tragedy. I loved Melissa despite of it all, for she had saved me from my death at such a young age, yet I couldn't shake the feeling that I was but a pawn in a game that I did not fully understand.

Another tale that Melissa would tell me, comes to mind...

'The year was 1523, and the French Quarter of New Orleans lay shrouded in the mist as the city clung to the edge of a swampy wilderness. The cobbled streets, narrow and winding, held secrets in their shadows, and the gas lamps cast long, flickering reflections in the dark waters of the bayou. It was a city where mysteries lingered in every corner, where life and death seemed to brush against one another, as close as lovers on a moonlit night. In the heart of this haunted city was Angelica, a creature as timeless as the ancient oaks that lined the streets, her existence a mystery known to a very few. She was a vampire, eternally beautiful, cursed with a hunger that could never be sated, yet driven by desires as human as those of the mortals who walked beneath her. Angelica's beauty was unmatched: skin pale as moonlight, eyes a haunting shade of deep amber, and long raven hair that cascaded over her shoulders like liquid silk. Her manner was elegant, her every movement deliberate and graceful, but there was an undeniable sadness in her eyes, an eternity of sorrow that no amount of time could ever erase. She had wandered the earth for centuries, moving through time as if it were a stolen dream, detached from the fleeting, mortal lives around her. In the French Quarter, she had found a home, a place where her otherworldly nature could hide among the eccentricities of the city. Here, no one questioned the woman who appeared only by night, her presence felt in the hushed whispers and the sudden chills that followed her, but one night, everything changed… It was a humid evening in late summer when Angelica first laid eyes on Marcus, a young and vibrant artist who had recently arrived from Paris. The son of a wealthy French merchant, Marcus had come to New Orleans seeking inspiration, drawn to the city by its vibrant culture and untamed beauty. He had taken residence in a small, sunlit apartment at the edge of the Quarter, where he spent his days painting scenes of the world he so desperately wanted to capture, and his nights wandering the streets in search of something he could not quite name. That night, Marcus found himself in Jackson Square, sitting beneath the towering Cathedral, sketching the world around him by the soft glow of the streetlamps. He was unaware that Angelica stood in the shadows, just watching him. She had sensed something different about him, something that drew her to him in a way she had not felt in centuries. There was a quiet intensity in his art, his work, a passion in his eyes that seemed to call out to her. Against her better judgement, Angelica found herself stepping closer, entranced by the man before her. As Marcus looked up, his gaze met hers, and for a moment, time itself seemed to stop. He had never seen a woman like her, ethereal, otherworldly, as if she had stepped out of one of his dreams. Her eyes held a depth he could not comprehend, and he felt an inexplicable pull toward her, as if the whole universe had suddenly shifted, drawing them together. Her beauty was very mesmerizing, Marcus was frozen at such a work of art, and his heart raced with inspiration at her mere p resence.

"Are you an artist, sir?" Angelica asked, her voice soft, comforting, yet filled with a quiet power.

Marcus nodded, struggling to find words in the presence of her beauty, her angelic frame, "I... I am, but I don't think I've ever captured anything as beautiful as you are, my lady."

A faint smile touched Angelica's lips, and for the first time in what felt like an eternity, she felt a spark of something she thought she had long forgotten, hope and love.

Over the weeks that followed, Angelica and Marcus saw each other often, their meetings always after the sun had set. Marcus, enraptured by her mysterious nature and exquisite beauty, could think of nothing else. He painted her endlessly, trying and failing to capture the enigmatic grace that seemed to flow from her every movement. In turn, Angelica found herself drawn to Marcus in ways she had never really experienced. His passion for life, his art, his kindness, all of it stirred with emotions within her long thought dead, but Angelica knew the dangers of allowing herself to love a mortal. Her curse was not just one of blood and hunger, but loneliness, an eternal existence in which love could only end in heartbreak of her undead heart. Still, she could not resist the inner feelings that blossomed deep inside her. For the first time in many centuries, she felt alive. Marcus, on the other hand, was falling hopelessly in love. He knew Angelica was unlike anyone he had ever met or seen, though he could not yet grasp the true extent of her nature. She was elusive, disappearing before dawn, avoiding sunlight as if it were a poison, but her voice, her laughter, her mere presence, these things consumed him. He spent hours painting her face, her eyes, her smile, always searching for something he could not name, something just beyond his reach. One night, as Marcus and Angelica walked along the misty banks of the Mississippi River, Marcus took her hand in his, he noticed the freezing chill of her hand, but ignored it, "Angelica," he began, his voice filled with intense emotion, "I feel like I've known you for forever, like my whole life has been leading to this moment. I don't know who you really are, or where you came from, but I do not care. All I know is that I have fallen for you, I am in love with you."

Angelica stopped, her amber eyes locking onto his. Her unbeaten heart, though long dead, seemed to ache in her cold chest. She had known this day would come, had feared it even as she longed for it. "Marcus," she whispered, her voice heavy with a hint of sadness, "There are things about me that you do not understand. I am not what you think I am."

He stepped closer, his gaze unwavering, "Then tell me. Let me understand. Whatever it is, it doesn't matter to me. I love you, Angelica, and nothing will change that."

For a long moment, Angelica was silent, torn between her inner desire to love and the need to protect him from the truth. Finally, she took a deep fake breath, and in that moment, the world around them seemed to grow still. "I am not like you," she said, her voice barely more than a whisper, "I am not human, a mortal. I have not been for centuries."

Marcus frowned, confusion flickering in his longing eyes, "What do you mean, Angelica?"

"I am a vampire, a blood sucking creature of the night," Angelica confessed, her words hanging in the air like the mere curse that she is,

"I have lived for over three hundred years, Marcus, sustained by the blood of the living. I am not human, and I never will be."

Marcus took a step back, his mind reeling. He stared at her, searching her face for some sign that she was only teasing him, but all he found was the cold, hard truth reflected in her eyes. His heart pounded in his chest as the weight of her words sank in, really sank deep within. "A vampire?" he repeated, his voice barely audible. "How... how is that even possible?"

"I do not expect you to understand, Marcus," Angelica said, her voice starting to tremble, "But it is the truth. I have lived many different lives over the centuries, and I have seen many things, but loving you... that is something I never thought possible within my undead heart, something I never thought I could actually do, could actually feel."

Marcus shook his head, struggling to process the revelation, "You... you actually drink blood? You actually kill people?"

Angelica's gaze dropped, her voice barely a whisper, "Yes, I have, but I have also learned to live without always killing. I do not take a human life unless I must."

For several moments, neither of them spoke, the silence between them filled with the sound of the river and the distant hum of the city. Finally, Marcus broke the silence, his voice filled with a mixture of fear and resolve. "I don't care, Angelica," he said, stepping closer to her, "I don't care what you are, whether you are a killer or not, I love you just the same. As I've already said, nothing will change that, my feelings still remain the same."

Angelica only stared at him, her unbeaten heart breaking and soaring at the same time. She wanted to believe him, wanted to believe that love could conquer even this, but deep down, she knew the truth. Their love was already doomed, destined to end in some type of tragedy. For a short time, Marcus and Angelica's love flourished in the darkness of the French Quarter. They met in secret, beneath the cover of the night, and those few precious hours together, they forgot the terrible truth that lay between them. Marcus, though still coming to terms with what Angelica was, could not deny the depth of his feelings for her. He loved her fiercely, completely, despite the danger that lurked in her freezing kiss, but Angelica knew their time together was fleeting. She had seen what happened to mortals who fell in love with vampires. She had watched them grow old while she remained unchanged, and she had witnessed the deep pain of watching them die while she lived on, cursed to remember them for eternity. She could not bear that same fate for Marcus. One night, as they lay together in her shadowy manor, nestled far from the bustling streets, Angelica turned to him, her heart heavy with the weight of the decision she had made, the decision to finally let him go. "We cannot continue like this, Marcus," she whispered as gently as she could, her voice thick with sorrow.

"Marcus frowned, pulling her closer, "What are you talking about, Angelica?"

"You are mortal." Angelica said, her voice trembling, "You will grow old, and I will remain as I am. I cannot watch you die, Marcus. I will not allow you to suffer because of me, besides, it's harder each night not to taste your pure blood coursing through your veins. It gets so tempting on some nights, and I do not want to ever harm you."

Marcus merely shook his head, his embrace tightening around her cold body, "I do not care about all that, Angelica. I don't care about growing old, all I want is to be with you for as long as I can."

"You just don't understand," Angelica pleaded, her voice breaking, "I have lived through this sort of thing before. I have watched people I loved once, die, while I remain, trapped in this existence. I cannot do it again, I should've known better than to ever fall in love with you."

Tears filled Marcus's eyes as he looked at her, his heart breaking. "Then make me what you are," he whispered, "Make me like you, immortal."

Angelica's eyes widened in horror, "No. I cannot do that. I will not place this curse upon you, I will not curse you with this life, you know not what you request of me."

"It's not a curse, Angelica," Marcus insisted, "It's the only way we can stay together, forever."

"No," Angelica said, pulling away from him, "You don't know what you are asking of me. This life... it's filled with much darkness, with hunger that will drive you mad, with endless suffering. I won't do that to you, Marcus. I love you too much."

Tears streamed down Marcu's face as he just stared at her, his heart shattering into a thousand pieces. "Then what are we supposed to do? Just let this come to an end? Let me grow old and die while you go on without me?"

Angelica closed her eyes, as a blood tear rolled down her pale, cold cheek, the pain of his words cutting deep, "I don't know," she whispered, "but I can't do this. I can't condemn you to this existence."

As the days passed, Marcus became consumed by his selfish desire to be with Angelica forever, his mind filled with the haunting knowledge that their time together was running out. He could not accept the idea of living without her now, he could not bear the thought of growing old while she remained ageless and perfect, with the grief of his death hanging within her frozen heart. The more he thought about all of it, the more his desperation grew, until it twisted into something darker. One night, Marcus went to the one place he knew he could find the answers he desired, the underground pits of the Quarter, where rumors of vampires lurked in the shadows. He did not care if it meant his life, he had to try. He had heard such rumors of the vampires' existence, whispered folk tales of those who could grant immortality to the willing, but with a price. And though Angelica had refused to turn him, Marcus believed that someone else might, especially after hearing their 'love' story. He found these vampires in the darkest corners of the city, a type of coven, ancient vampires led by a cruel and powerful figure named Leroy, unlike Angelica, who had learned to temper her hunger, Leroy reveled in the violence and bloodlust that came with being an immortal creature of the night. Leroy saw mortals as nothing more than prey, and when Marcus came to him with his bizarre request, Leroy saw an opportunity, "You wish to be turned into what we are?" Leroy asked, his voice dripping with much malice.

Marcus nodded, his heart racing in his chest, "Yes, I need to be turned, to be with her, my love, Angelica, I cannot live without her."

Leroy smiled, his fangs glinting in the dim light, "And does she request this also, does she know you are here? Does she know you have come to me?"

Marcus hesitated, guilt gnawing at him, "No, but she will have to understand. Once, I am like her, she'll accept my fate."

Leroy chuckled darkly, circling Marcus like a hungry predator, "Ah, such young, determined love. So blind, so foolish. Very well, my mere mortal, I will give you what you seek."

Without warning, Leroy lunged at Marcus, sinking his fangs deep into his neck. The pain was excruciating, but Marcus welcomed it, believing that it would bring him closer to Angelica, that it would let them remain together for all eternity, never allowing such sorrow of loss again for her. He felt his life slipping away, replaced by something dark and ancient, something that twisted and burned inside him, as he drank a cup of warm, thick blood from Leroy. When the transformation was complete, Marcus stumbled back, his body shaking, his senses heightened. He could feel the hunger swelling, rising within him, the thirst for blood, but all he could think of was Angelica, how she would now have no reason to reject his love, how they could be together for eternity now. But when he returned to her later that night, everything fell apart. Angelica was waiting for him, her heart heavy with an unknown dread. She had felt something shift in the air, the city, a darkness creeping closer, and when Marcus stepped through the faded door, she knew immediately what he had done. His blood smelled different, his scent was as a dead creature, immortal. "No," she whispered, her voice filled with horror, defeat, "What have you done, Marcus?"

Marcus stood before her, his eyes wild, his body trembling with the new power coursing through him, "I did this for you, for us, Angelica," he said, his voice filled with desperation, "I did this so we could stay together forever."

Angelica shook her head, blood tears streaming down her face, "You don't understand, you've doomed us both. I can smell the blood within you, the blood of a monster."

Before Marcus could respond, Leroy appeared in the faint doorway, a sinister smile on his face, "You didn't think I would merely let you have him all to yourself for eternity, did you, Angelica?"

Angelica's blood ran cold as she realized the full extent of the betrayal. Leroy had used Marcus to get to her, had turned him not out of kindness, but to bind him to his dark tangled web. Marcus was no longer hers, he now belonged to Leroy, to the darkness that had consumed him. Leroy once wanted her for himself, but she escaped and stayed hidden from his grasp, but now he was here to claim them both. "Marcus," Angelica whispered, her undead heart shattering, "You've become someone, something, I can never love. You are now his, bound to him by his sadistic blood. Leroy will never allow you to be free from his grasp."

Marcus's face crumpled with anguish as the truth of her words sank in. He had thought immortality would keep them together forever, but it had only torn them apart. "I'm so sorry, my love," he whispered, faintly, falling to his knees before her, "I am so sorry."

But it was too late now, the damage was done, and there was no going back. Angelica, her undead heart broken, turned away from him, the love they had once shared now lost to the darkness forever.

Angelica left New Orleans that very night, disappearing quickly into the shadows of the massive world, leaving behind the only love she had known in many centuries. She wandered the earth alone, haunted by the memory of Marcus, the man she had once loved and lost to the immortal darkness, the wretched curse of immortality. Marcus, now bound by Leroy's blood, lived on in New Orleans, for he could never leave, yet he was a shadow of the man he had once been. He roamed the streets of the French Quarter, searching for Angelica in every face, every whisper, but he never found her. The immortality he had sought had become his prison, and the love he had fought for was now nothing more than a distant, painful memory. Marcus realized that Angelica had spoken the truth, it was a curse, and it was for all eternity. And so, their tragic love story became a legend, whispered among the hidden vampires of the French Quarter, a tale of love, jealousy, and betrayal, of a love that could never be, and the darkness that consumed them both for all eternity.'

This estranged, tragic romance, that Melissa spoke of to me that night, still dwells in my thoughts, heavy, with such sorrow for a love that could never have been, whether it was true or not.

With time, the brothel house transformed into the majestic hotel, that now stands proudly in the French Quarter, a blend of my past and my present. I filled these walls with memories of joy, a stark contrast to the blood-soaked history that lay beneath. The hotel became a symbol of my survival, an attempt to reclaim my mere identity amidst the chaos of my immortal existence, and as I moved through these very halls, I sometimes see the ghost of Melissa, in the corner of my eyes, like a fleeting shadow, darting from one room to the next, a reminder of the choice that shaped me. The strange habits of Melissa that had once exhibited still linger in my mind, and I often found myself wondering if she too had felt the weight of her immortality, of her cruel actions, and the burden of immortality pressing down on her undead heart. Now, as I reflect on those past moments, I realize that our lives were forever intertwined, never to be apart, a tapestry woven with threads of love, loss, and the haunting echoes of our regrets. Melissa will for all eternity remain in this place and in my thoughts.

The memories of my transformation, so long ago, will always linger, a constant reminder of the fine line I walk between the dark shadows and the pale light, as I continue to contemplate the complexities of my immortal existence.

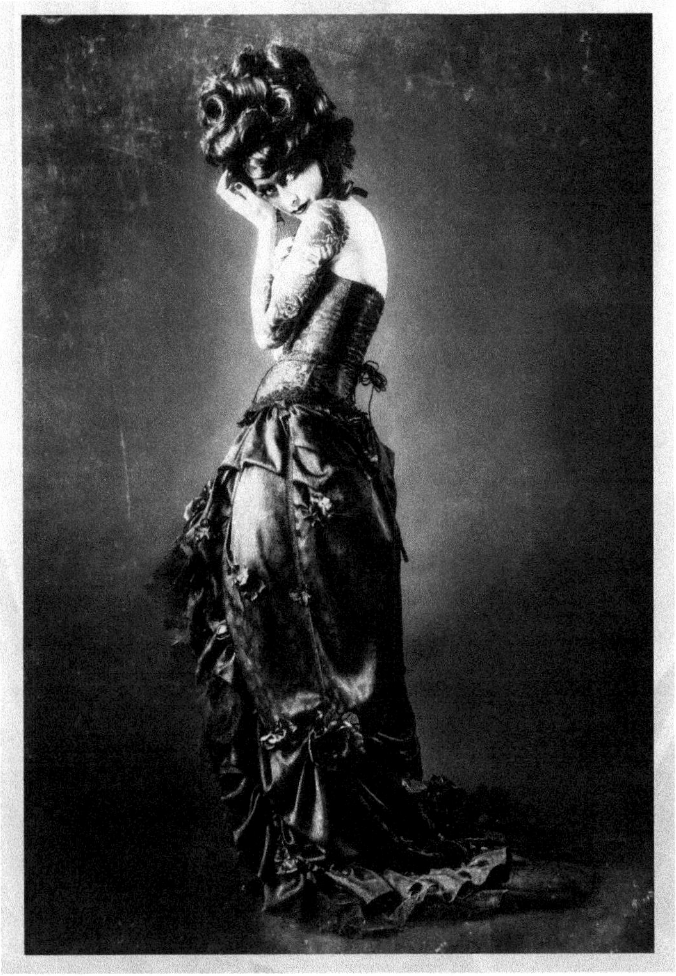

Chapter 4

Gazing from my discreet window in my hotel room, the soft glow of twilight spills into the room, casting long shadows that dance across the floor. The air is thick with the scents of jasmine and dampened earth, and I can't help but let my mind drift back to the good times, the better moments, shared with Melissa within these walls that was once a brothel house. Those moments were often eclipsed by a form of darkness, but there were flickers of light that punctuated our existence, conversations that left its mark on my undead soul, shaping the very essence of who I became.

I remember evenings when we would settle into the plush armchairs in the parlor, while the brothel house was quiet and secluded, the air heavy with the scent of incense and the warm glow of faint candlelight. Melissa would pour us each a glass of dark red wine, her movements graceful and fluid, and she would begin to weave her small stories, captivating me with tales of romance and intimate tragedy. I reflect back on one such tale that she told me...

'"Once, there was a beautiful, lady vampire called Elizabeth," Melissa would start her story, her eyes glinting with a mixture of nostalgia and sorrow. "She fell in love with a mortal man, a poet whose words could make the stars weep. Their love was passionate but doomed from the very start, for Elizabeth knew that to embrace him would mean dragging him into the depths of mere darkness with her."

Her voice would take on a melodic quality, painting vivid images in my mind. I could actually see images of this Elizabeth, ethereal and tragic, a woman trapped between two worlds. Melissa continued her tale, "In a moment of desperation, Elizabeth turned him, making him immortal, same as her, but he lost himself in the blood hunger, overwhelmed by the desire to feed. He became a monster, and Elizabeth was left alone to wander the lonely nights, burdened by her love for a man who could no longer recognize her. She must carry on in her eternity regretting her choices."'

These stories were always steeped with pain and longing, reflections of Melissa's own experiences, and I often could feel a slight connection to them. Although, she would never tell me her true story of her past, yet I knew she suffered loss and heartbreak. I could hear her silent pain in every word she spoke as she told her tales to me. Each tale resonated with my heart, echoing the fears I silently harbored about my own fate, my unknown future, "Melissa, do you believe in love at all? Do you believe in a love that transcends any type of darkness?" I once asked her, my voice barely above a whisper.

"Love is the only thing that can save us from ourselves, Maria Grace, yet it can also be the very thing that leads us into bitter despair," Melissa replied, her gaze distant as if she were peering into a past that was both beautiful and heart-wrenching. "We must be careful whom we choose to truly love, for in this life, every connection comes with a price. Human beings must believe in some type of love, some form of hope, and some means of an eternity, whether it's Heaven or Hell, or any type of religious beliefs, otherwise, one would go insane, giving up on life completely."

Those quiet evenings were filled with small giggles and many shared secrets of emotion, a balm against the burdens we carried deep within. In Melissa's presence, I found a sense of belonging, a shared understanding that transcended the worldly realm of our reality in this brothel house. We would talk late into the night, the essence of the faint candlelight casting various shadows that seemed to dance across the walls, as she would speak of the eternal struggles of make-believe immortals, of lost souls seeking some form of love, some form of redemption. One night, our conversation turned to deeper matters, faith, religion, and the concepts of Heaven and Hell. I was intrigued yet confused, caught in a crossroads of my own beliefs, "Do you think there is a God? I asked instantly, unsure of how she would respond.

"God is there, Maria Grace, much like immortality, He never dies," Melissa would muse, her voice thoughtful, "Some would say individuals are cursed to roam this earth for an eternity, yet others believe God would take them sooner because He needs them in Heaven. Some souls are left here to roam this planet without any purpose, while other souls become a part of a grander design, chosen to bear the weight of the world, as if forever. Heaven and Hell are real, depending on our choices we make during our life, that is what determines one's fate, a reflection of our choices is what manifests our souls."

"But what of redemption?" I pressed, yearning for clarity on the subject, "Can we ever atone for the lives we've decided to live? The darkness within that so many people carry?"

Melissa's expression softened, and for a brief moment, I saw a ray of vulnerability in her emerald eyes, "Redemption is merely a journey, I think, Maria Grace, not a destination. Every decision we make shapes our path, whether good or bad, we may not find absolution, but we can seek understanding. In the end of one's journey, it's the love we share, however fleeting, that grants us a semblance of any type of peace. Some will find it, and some will remain wandering, searching, for an eternity."

Melissa's words hung in the air, resonating deeply inside me. Although, I did not fully understand her meaning at the time, I realize now exactly what she was trying to say to me. Her words were haunting yet comforting, filling the void left by my fragmented understanding of such matters. I yearned for her wisdom on these subjects, yet I knew that my own path was destined to be fraught with dim shadows surrounding my soul.

There's been many moments where I missed hearing Melissa's voice, I would find myself missing her more than I cared to admit. After taking her life, an emptiness settled within me, a small void that echoed with memories we shared and all the heartfelt conversations that were spoken between us. I had ended her existence, and I pondered some nights, if she found her redemption, her Heaven or Hell. I couldn't shake the feeling that I also severed a vital part of myself, the night Melissa ceased to exist.

Another story surfaces in my mind, that Melissa told me...

'Savannah in the early 1500's was a city cloaked in beauty and contradiction, where cobblestone streets meandered beneath towering magnolia trees, and the scent of blooming jasmine drifted through the air. The city was young, built on dreams of prosperity, but beneath its facade of elegance and wealth, secrets festered. It was in this city, so full of charm yet plagued by shadows, that a young woman named

Sophia found herself caught in a web of desire, faith, and heartbreak. Sophia was the daughter of a modest preacher, raised with the virtues of humility and piety instilled in her from a young age. Her father's voice echoed in her mind daily, reminding her that a woman's place was one of modesty, servitude to God, and devotion to righteousness, but Savannah, with its wealth and social intricacies, offered temptations that even the most devout could not always resist. Sophia was a striking beauty, though she never saw herself as such. Her hair was a deep chestnut, curling around her face in soft waves, and her eyes were as blue as the Atlantic Ocean that bordered her world. Yet her beauty was marred by an inner turmoil, a constant battle between what she knew to be right and what her heart yearned for. This conflict began the day she met Thomas.

Thomas was a man of status and influence, married to a woman named Stella, one of Savannah's wealthiest women. Stella was everything that Savannah valued, elegant, sophisticated, and deeply tied to the old money that ran through the veins of the city. Their marriage, while politically advantageous, was anything but passionate. Stella's heart was as cold as the diamonds she wore, and her eyes, though often filled with desire for control and status, held little warmth for her husband. Sophia first saw Thomas during one of Savannah's social gatherings, an elaborate fete held beneath the grand oaks of Forsyth Park. He was standing near the fountain, his dark hair falling in soft waves, his tall frame silhouetted against the sunset. There was something about him, an air of quiet intelligence, a restlessness in his gaze that seemed to mirror her own. When their eyes met across the crowded lawn, Sophia felt an undeniable pull toward him, as though the universe had shifted and brought them together in that single moment, a chemistry so strong swirling through the air. They spoke for the first time that evening, when fate, or perhaps something more, guided her to him. Sophia had been helping her mother with charitable work, serving food to the poor of the city, when Thomas approached. He was courteous, polite, but his eyes lingered on her in a way that made her feel seen, truly seen, for the first time in her life. "You have a kind heart, miss," Thomas said softly, in a flirtatious manner, as she handed a bowl of soup to a beggar.

Sophia's heart raced at the mere sound of his voice, "I only do what is right, sir," she replied, though her hands trembled slightly.

Thomas smiled, but there was sadness in his eyes, "Sometimes what is right is not what we truly desire."

The words struck Sophia, resonating with a truth she had been trying to deny. Over the coming weeks, their paths crossed more frequently. Savannah was small, after all, and Sophia found herself attending more gatherings where Thomas was present. Each time they met, their conversations grew deeper, more intimate, until Sophia found herself falling in love with a man, she knew she could never have. Sophia's love for Thomas became a torment, a constant struggle between her religious beliefs and the strong desires that consumed her. Every time she saw him, her heart ached with such longing, but her conscience reminded her that he was a married man. To give in to her feelings would be a great sin, a betrayal of everything she had been taught. She sought solace in the church, kneeling for hours before the sacred altar, praying for strength to resist the temptation that had taken root in her heart. The image of Christ on the cross loomed above her, a reminder of the sacrifices she was expected to make in this life, and yet, no matter how hard she prayed, the feelings did not fade. "Forgive me, Lord," she whispered, her voice breaking with emotion, "I know what is right, but my heart... my heart does not obey."

Her father, sensing the changes in her demeanor, grew concerned. He had always been a stern, honest man, his faith unwavering, and he feared for his daughter's soul. He noticed how she would often gaze out the window with a faraway look, her mind clearly elsewhere, and how her once cheerful spirit seemed weighed down by some unseen burden. "Sophia," her father said one evening, as they sat by the fire in their modest home, "Is there something troubling you?"

Sophia hesitated, her heart pounding in her chest. She truly wanted to confess, to tell him of the storm that raged within her, but she feared his reaction. How could she explain that she had fallen in love with a man who was bound by marriage to another? "I... I am struggling with my faith, Father," she finally answered, her voice barely above a whisper, "There are feelings I have that I know are wrong, but I cannot make them go away."

Her father's brow furrowed with concern, but his voice remained calm, "The Lord tests us in many ways, Sophia. He puts obstacles in our path to see if we will remain true to Him. You must trust in God's plan, even when it is difficult."

Sophia nodded, but her heart felt heavy. How could this be part of God's plan? How could a love that felt so pure, so right, be so wrong? One evening, as the sun dipped below the horizon, casting a warm glow over the city. Sophia found herself wandering through the garden of one of Savannah's grand estates. It was quiet, the guests still inside, and the only sound was the rustle of the wind through the magnolia trees. She had come here to escape, to clear her mind, but instead, she found herself thinking of only Thomas, and then, as if summoned by her thoughts, he appeared in her path. "Sophia," he said softly, his voice causing her heart to leap in her chest. She could see him standing there, his expression unreadable, but his eyes filled with the same longing she had tried so desperately to suppress. "Thomas," she whispered, unable to hide the tremble in her voice, "You shouldn't be here."

"I had to see you," Thomas said, stepping closer, "I can't stop thinking about you, Sophia. Every moment we are apart feels like an eternity."

Sophia felt her resolve crumbling. His words echoed the very thoughts that had plagued her, and in that moment, the weight of her inner conflict felt too much to bear. "This is wrong," she said, though her voice lacked the conviction, "You are married. This would only be lust, not fully love. We cannot..."

"I know," Thomas interrupted, his voice filled with anguish, "But my marriage... it is not what you think. Stella and I... we were never in love with each other. It was arranged, a matter of business, of combining wealth. I have never felt for Stella what I feel for you, what I feel every time I see you."

Sophia's heart raced, torn between the love she felt for him and the guilt that gnawed at her, "But it does not matter, sir," she said, tears welling in her eyes, "You are bound to her, in the eyes of God and the law."

Thomas reached for her hand, his touch sending a jolt of electricity through her body, "Does it matter to God that we love each other? That I have found in you what I never thought possible?"

His words broke through the barriers she had built around her heart, and for the first time, Sophia allowed herself to imagine a world where they could actually be together, but the reality of their situation weighed heavily on her. "I don't know the answer to your question, sir," Sophia whispered, her voice filled with despair, "I do not know what is right anymore."

Thomas pulled her into his arms, holding her close as she wept warm tears down her fragile face. For a moment, they stood there beneath the magnolia trees, lost in each other, the world around them fading into nothing, but even as their hearts beat in unison, the shadows of their forbidden love loomed over them, threatening to tear them apart before they had even begun. Days turned into weeks, and Sophia and Thomas continued to see each other in secret, their love growing stronger with each stolen moment, but the guilt weighed more heavily on Sophia's soul, and no matter how much she tried to justify her feelings, she could not escape the knowledge that their love was built on lies and deception. She knew deep within that Thomas would never fully be hers, he would never actually be her husband. It wasn't long before the rumors began to spread. Savannah was a small city, and people talked. Sophia noticed the way the other ladies would look at her, especially during church services, their whispers barely concealed. She could feel the bitter judgement in their eyes, could hear the condemnation in their hushed voices. Thomas's wife, Stella, too, had begun to suspect that something was amiss. Stella was not a woman easily fooled, and though her marriage to Thomas was one of convenience, she still took pride in the status it afforded her. The idea that her husband might be unfaithful was an insult to her pride, and she would not tolerate it. One evening, as Sophia made her way home from one of her clandestine meetings with Thomas, she was stopped by a woman she recognized from church, Agnes, a notorious gossip. "Sophia," Agnes said, her voice dripping with false concern, "I've heard some troubling things about you, my dear. People are talking, you know. They say you've been seen with Sir Thomas."

Sophia's heart raced with fright, her face flushing with shame, "I... I don't know what you are speaking about," she stammered.

Agnes smiled, her eyes gleaming with malice, "Oh, I think you do, my dear. And so does Stella."

Sophia felt a wave of panic wash over her. If Stella knew, then it was only a matter of time before the truth would come out. Her mere reputation, her family's name, her father's reputation as a preacher, everything she worked so hard to protect would be ruined. It wasn't long before the confrontation she had feared came to pass. One evening, as Sophia was returning home from a secret meeting with Thomas, she found Stella waiting for her on the porch of her father's house. Stella's face was a mask of cold fury, her eyes blazing with hatred. "So, it's true," Stella said, her voice low and dangerous, "You've been seeing my husband."

Sophia felt her heart drop. She had known this moment would eventually come, but now that it was here, she felt utterly unprepared. "Stella, please," she began, her voice trembling with fear and guilt, "It's not exactly what you think..."

Stella laughed, a bitter sound, "Oh, I think it's exactly what I think. You've been sneaking around with my Thomas behind my back, haven't you? You think because you're so young and pretty, you can steal my husband from me?"

Sophia's eyes filled with regretful tears, guilt and shame overwhelming her, "I'm sorry," she murmured, her voice breaking, "I never meant for any of this to happen."

"Sorry?" Stella spat, her face twisted with much anger, "You will be sorry. I will ruin you, Miss Sophia, I will make sure everyone in Savannah knows what kind of woman you really are."

Sophia felt a wave of shame and despair wash over her. She had just lost everything, her mere reputation as a woman, her faith, her love. There was no escape from the consequences of her actions. After the confrontation with Stella, Thomas and Sophia's world began to crumble. The rumors spread like wildfire, and soon, Sophia found herself shunned by the very community that had once embraced her. Women whispered about her in church, men no longer offered her the polite respect they once had, and her father, devastated by the shame she had brought upon their family, could barely look at her.

Thomas, too, found himself trapped in a prison of his own making. His marriage to Stella, though, loveless, was bound by the expectations of wealth and society. To leave her for Sophia would mean financial ruin, not just for himself, but for his family, and though his heart ached for Sophia, he knew, now, that he could never truly be with her. Their love, once filled with hope and passion, had become a source of pain and regret. They met one final time, beneath the magnolia trees where their love had first blossomed. The air was heavy with the scent of flowers, but the beauty of the moment was lost beneath the weight of their sorrow. "I'm so sorry, Sophia," Thomas stated, his voice thick with much emotion, "I wish things could be different."

Sophia nodded, warm tears streaming down her face, "I already know, Thomas," she said, her voice barely audible, "but they cannot be different."

For a long moment, they stood in mere silence, the reality of their situation sinking in. There was no future for them, no happy ending. Their love, though pure in heart, was doomed from the start. "I will always love you, Sophia," Thomas said, his voice breaking.

"And I you, Thomas," Sophia replied, her heart shattering with every word.

With one final, lingering, heated kiss, Sophia and Thomas parted, knowing they would never see each other again. Sophia watched as Thomas disappeared into the night, his tall figure fading into the shadows, leaving her alone beneath the magnolia trees. In the months that followed, Sophia's life became a shell of what it had once been. The weight of her guilt and shame pressed down on her, cruelly, and though she sought solace in the church, she found no comfort. Her once unshakable faith had been fractured by the choices she had made, and she could no longer reconcile the religious teachings of her childhood with the desires of her broken heart. Her father, heartbroken by the whole scandal, withdrew from his duties as a preacher, unable to face the judgement of the community. Sophia's family became pariahs, and the once modest but happy life they had led was destroyed. Sophia tried to move on, to find peace in the knowledge that she had loved, even if it ended in tragedy, embarrassment, but the memories of Thomas still haunted her, and the knowledge that their love had been wrong, at least in the eyes of God and society, tormented her soul. As the years passed, Sophia withdrew from the world, retreating into herself, her once bright spirit dimmed by the weight of her poor choices. She never married; never found the happiness she had longed for. Instead, she lived out her days in quiet solitude, her heart forever marked by the love she had lost, the love she could never have, and though, she prayed for forgiveness, for redemption, she could never fully rid herself of the feeling that, in choosing to love Thomas, she had lost not just him, but herself. In the end, the magnolia trees of Savannah stood as silent witnesses to their tragic love, a love that could never be, yet one that would never be forgotten.'

I reflect back on the mornings I spent in the quiet of my room in the brothel house, reading poetry and various parchments of papers on many different subjects, the sun rising over the rooftops of New Orleans, as I shared a peaceful breakfast with myself. It would be hours before laughter filled the place downstairs, as I felt the weight of loneliness creep in, awaiting the moment at dusk when Melissa would surface from her room. I did miss the simplicity of those early days with her. Yet, alongside the fond memories, there was an undercurrent of many regrets that gnawed at me. I had made a choice in a moment of rage and desperation, a choice that had irrevocably altered the course of my life. 'Could there have been another way? Could I have saved Melissa instead of ending her undead life?' These thoughts often lingered in the corners of my mind, shrouded in a veil of melancholy. I had been so blinded by my pain of losing Patrick, and learning of my mother's death, that I had failed to recognize the depth of Melissa's own struggles, her pain. As I stared into this vintage, silver mirror, that was given to me by Melissa, I saw not just my own reflection, but the echoes of a love forever lost, one that had shaped my very being. 'Could I have ever forgiven her for the things, the pain, she caused me?'

In the silence of my hotel, I allowed myself to reminisce, to celebrate the bond we once shared while acknowledging the darker path that was laid before me. The memories, the few laughs we shared, the late-night conversations, the tales she told, and the shared sorrows intertwined like vines around my undead heart, a testament to the complex relationship I had built with Melissa amidst the shadows of a darkened era. And, as I continued my eternal journey of my own existence, I hoped that I could find a small ray of peace, both for myself and for the ghost of Melissa that still lingered within me, a reminder of the vague love we had once, a love that burned with a dim fire, now forever entwined with the mystery of our shared fate.

Chapter 5

As I reflect back on being in the dimly lit parlor of the brothel house, surrounded by the weight of its history and the faint scent of incense, that Melissa always burned throughout the place, I found solace in a world woven from mere words. It was here, amidst the plush velvet cushions and burning candles, that Melissa introduced me to the art of dark poetry, a realm where souls could wander freely, unencumbered by the burdens of our mere existence. I remember the first time she handed me a worn leather notebook with stained parchment paper, its pages yellowed and frayed at the edges. "This is where the shadows whisper, Maria Grace," Melissa would say, her voice a soft melody that wrapped around me like a warm embrace. "Write what you feel, my sweet dear, let your heart bleed onto the pages."

Her encouragement ignited a fire within me, we would spend countless evenings nestled in those velvet chairs, the air thick with much creativity as I scribbled my thoughts and emotions into the pages, along with many of the words that Melissa would quote. Melissa would craft her own verses onto these pages, her feathered pen gliding effortlessly across the yellowed paper. The atmosphere was charged with a sense of respect and understanding, a sacred space where our fears and inner desires coalesced into something beautiful.

As I dwell here in the silence of my hotel room, I still look upon these ancient pages of this leather notebook with its faded yellowed paper, a cherished piece of the days long gone. I remember Melissa's words, "Poetry is a reflection of our souls," she would say, her emerald eyes alight with passion, "It allows us to confront the darkest of nights, to find meaning in our pain. Each line is a piece of us, a glimpse into the depths of our mere being."

As I reflect on this memory of Melissa, my mind reminds me of the one night that Melissa had told me a couple of silly fairytales...

'The moon hung like a ghostly lantern over the darkened woods, casting silvery threads of light through the skeletal trees. Deep within the shadowed heart of the hidden forest, where few dared to venture, stood a clearing veiled in mist. Here, beneath ancient oaks and whispering willows, was where she awaited him, Elara, a creature of twilight and dew, a fairy whose wings shimmered like stars caught in the grip of midnight. She was radiant, luminous in a way that defied nature and was intoxicating. Her skin held the glow of moonlight, and her eyes reflected the depth of secret skies. To any human eyes, she was a vision beyond imagination, ethereal and otherworldly. Nicholas, a young man of no particular renown, had met Elara by a twist of fate, or perhaps fate had intended their paths to cross, though foe what purpose neither dared to guess. Each night he crept away from the boundaries of the small village, past high wooden walls meant to protect, into the hidden woods that was forbidden by the people of the village to ever enter. The officials of the village warned him of creatures that lured men to ruin, of enchantresses who promised Heaven but delivered Hell, yet, Nicholas came, drawn by the force he could not name, an ache he could not deny. As he entered the clearing within the hidden forest, his breath caught. Elara was waiting, her wings a soft glow in the thick mist. She smiled, that smile that seemed to hold both joy and sorrow. Nicholas approached her, the leaves crunching underfoot. "Elara," he whispered, his voice a blend of wonder and true longing, "I am here."

Elara reached out, her hand barely grazing his cheek. Her touch was cool, like the first breath of dawn. "You shouldn't have come here, Nicholas."

"But how could I not?" He replied, his eyes searching hers, filled with unspoken promises. "My heart belongs only to you, Elara."

Elara closed her fragile eyes, pained. "You world... and mine... they are not meant to touch, to combine. The elders of my world say I will fade if I remain too long in the world of men." Her voice trembled, breaking slightly. "And you will age, Nicholas. You will grow old, and I ..."

Nicholas silenced her with a warm kiss, capturing the sadness in her words, sealing them away. They stood entwined, two unmatching souls cleaving together against the weight of their much different worlds. Elara pulled back, her breath like a song lingering in the damp, cool air. "If they find out, they will tear us apart, Nicholas. They will drag me back to my hidden world of fairies, and you... they will see you as a threat."

"What threat am I, Elara?" he asked bitterly. "I am just a man who dared to love a beautiful creature too wondrous for words."

A gust of wind rustled the trees around them, as if the forest itself whispered warnings. Elara's wings trembled; their glow flickered as her resolve faltered. She knew the elders had grown suspicious; they had begun watching her closely, sensing her straying from the path that was destined for her. "You must go, Nicholas," Elara murmured, tears glistening in her eyes, "If we are discovered, they will show no mercy. They will erase all memory of me from your human mind."

"Let them try," Nicholas replied fiercely, "You are burned into my soul. They could strip the stars from the sky, and I would still remember your light, the glow of your wings, and the sparkle of your fragile eyes."

Elara shivered, clutching his hand as if to hold him there, to bridge the chasm between them, but she knew the night was nearing its end, and her kind could not remain under human skies come dawn. If she lingered too long, she would lose herself in his world, become a mere shadow of what she was as a fairy, a faint glimmer until she finally faded. A sudden crack of branches startled them both. Figures emerged from the faint darkness, tall, spectral beings, their eyes cold as the moon above. The supreme elders of Elara's realm had come for her, their colorful cloaks trailing like whispers over the ground. "Enough," one of the elders intoned, his voice hollow and ancient, "You have broken the laws of our kind, Elara. The human world is not ours to dwell within, and you, mortal..." The elder turned his daring gaze to Nicholas, "you will forget her, you will lose all memory of Elara after this night."

"No!" Elara cried out, clinging to Nicholas, but her form was already beginning to blur, as if caught between worlds. She reached for him, her fingers slipping like mist through his.

"Elara!" Nicholas choked, his voice breaking as he tried to yell, "Don't leave me, not like this!"

But the elders pulled her back as she flickered, their hands raised, weaving fairy spells as old as time. She gazed at him one last time, her face etched with anguish, her form fading like the last glimmers of a dying star.

"I will always remember you, Elara." Nicholas whispered, his words a plea, a promise.

And then, Elara was gone, as well as all the elders. They were safe within their hidden world.

As dawn broke over the abandoned forest, Nicholas fell to his knees, staring at the empty space where Elara had stood. His heart felt hollow, as if a part of him had been torn away. The village would soon stir, and he would return, carrying the ghost of a love much forbidden, a love lost to him, lost to the edges of merely a myth, and each night, he would come to the clearly of the hidden forest hoping, waiting, calling out a name he could not remember who she was, Elara. Shouting it into the endless silence, knowing in his soul that someone by this name meant something to him, and that she was somewhere beyond, listening to his cries.'

The other fantasy tale that Melissa quoted to me...

'The land of Eirwald was wild and treacherous, with misty hills and ancient forests that whispered of magic and mystery. In the far reaches of the mountains, where only the bravest dared to wander, lived a dragon, a creature as ancient as the land itself. His massive scales shimmered with hues of midnight and steel, and his large eyes held the wisdom of many centuries. He was a fierce protector of the wild lands, a silent guardian of many secrets buried deep in shadow, but he was not a creature devoid of heart. His soul, though armored by scales and fire, was very tender, and in time, it came to love a human woman, a love that was like loving as a father to its child. Her name was Althea, a woman of spirit and grace, with hair the color of autumn leaves and eyes like green woodland pools. She had first encountered the dragon in the quiet of the mountains, a fateful meeting under a sky heavy with rain. Strangely afraid, she'd approached the majestic beast, a magical creature, her heart drawn to his silent strength and watchful gaze. Althea had wandered too far away as she daydreamed, with the heavy rains closing in she needed shelter, that's when she found the dragon, nestled in a large, damp cave. In her presence, the dragon felt a peace he hadn't known in ages. Their unique connection deepened with every meeting, thereafter, bound by unspoken understanding and a shared sense of inner loneliness. But another man, one of the village hunters, was also drawn to Althea. His name was Rhys, a handsome man with a charm that masked something darker. He was ambitious, covetous, and saw Althea as a prize to possess rather than a soul to cherish. Rhys's obsession with Althea grew, and when he discovered that she ventured to the mountains frequently to meet the dragon, a hint of jealousy twisted his heart. To him, the dragon was a rival, a monster keeping him from what he desired most. Rhys had warned her, "That creature, that fierce dragon, is extrememly dangerous, Althea. It will turn on you one day; dragons are beasts of fire and much hunger, not loyalty."

But Althea only shook her head, "You do not understand, Rhys. He has never harmed me. He only wants my true friendship and to protect me, to protect these lands, and he... he is more noble than you can imagine."

Rhys's gaze darkened, "You are blinded by a creature, a beast, that cares for nothing but its own power."

That night, as Althea returned from her routinely visit to the mountains, she found Rhys waiting for her by her cottage. His demeanor was strangely different, colder, and his eyes glinted with something very menacing. "He won't allow us to be together," Rhys said, his voice low and bitter. "That beast has poisoned your mind against, I just know it. That creature needs to be dead."

Althea took a step back, suddenly uneasy, "It isn't like that, Rhys. The dragon is my friend, my protector. There's a darkness in you that he has seen, that I've started to see too."

At her words, Rhys's face contorted with rage. Before she could react, Rhys lunged, his hands reaching for her with an intent far from love, but in that moment, a massive shadow descended, and the ground shook as a mighty roar echoed across the valley. The dragon had arrived, his scales gleaming in the moonlight like armor. Rhys froze, his face twisting in terror. With a single swipe of the dragon's massive tail, it sent Rhys sprawling. He turned to Althea, his gaze softening, urging her to stay back. She watched, her heart pounding, torn between horror and relief as the dragon defended her, revealing its true nature. For he had known of Rhys's inner darkness, had sensed the cruelty masked by the man's charm. Rhys stumbled to his feet, regaining his composure, clutching a dagger, "You'll pay for this, you monster," he spat, lunging at the dragon in desperation.

But the dragon's claws met Rhys's advance, ending it in a swift, final blow. Silence fell over the clearing, near the cottage where Althea stood, her body trembling, her heart aching with horrified grief, for despite everything, she had slightly cared for Rhys once. The dragon, her silent sentinel, gazed at her, sorrow evident in his ancient eyes. He had spared her from a life bound to a man of hidden malice, yet he knew the pain his actions had just caused her. As the dawn broke over the hills, she knelt by the dragon's side, resting her hand on his scaled neck. "You saw his inner darkness when I could not," Althea whispered, her voice breaking, "And yet... my heart feels broken."

The dragon lowered his head, his soft rumble a sound of regret and much understanding. He had hoped to protect her from harm, even if it meant bearing her sorrow in his magical heart. Though words were beyond him, his eyes held a silent promise: he would remain her sole protector, her friend, always, guarding her from dangers she might never see. For in Althea's heartache, she might one day find healing, nut the dragon would forever be bound to her, a creature of flame and loyalty in a world that did not understand such devotion.'

Melissa often shared her own works of poetry with me, poems steeped in the themes of love, loss, and the bittersweet nature of one's immortality. "Listen," she would say, as she began, her voice low and melodic, reciting the lines that lingered in the air long after she had spoken them...

"In shadows deep, where secrets dwell,

I walk the line of Heaven and Hell,

With fangs of longing and a heart of stone,

I wander through darkness, forever alone."

The verses flowed from her lips like a haunting lullaby, resonating within my soul, awakening something I hadn't yet understood. Each word carried the weight of her experiences, encapsulating the very essence of her immortal life, yet I was unaware of such at that time. I would sit, enraptured, as she unveiled the layers of her soul through her poetry, the connection between us deepening with every shared moment. As the nights stretched into weeks, I began to find my own voice of poetry. Melissa guided me with gentle encouragement, helping me shape my raw emotions into verses that spoke to the shadows I held within, as I would scribble the words onto the yellowed paper, she would say, "Let your pain, your joy, your deepest feelings become your art."

As I wrestled with my inner feelings trying to place them onto the pages, Melissa would whisper as she watched, "Transform all the dark emotions into something bright, something beautiful."

One night in particular surfaces in my mind, the moon was casting a silvery glow through the stained-glass window, illuminating the parlor with an ethereal light. Melissa and I sat across from each other, the silence punctuated only by the sound of our feathered pens scratching against the faded pages. I felt a surge of inspiration and began to read my latest creation of words aloud, my voice trembling but determined...

"In the depths of night, I wander lost,

Haunted by echoes, the shadows embossed,

The love that slipped through my trembling hands,

Leaving me adrift on forgotten sands."

Melissa listened intently at my words, a proud smile gracing her lips, "Beautiful, Maria Grace," she said, her voice thick with emotion. "You capture the essence of longing so perfectly in those words, your pain seemed apart of you, yet it does not define you. Your words are much more than sorrowful."

Those peaceful moments, surrounded by the comforts of such words, forged a deeper bond between us that made us feel safe, secure. Poetry became our refuge, a sanctuary where we could express our innermost thoughts without having to relate our full meaning, without fear of judgement. We shared our hopes and fears through the verses of poetry we created, breathing life into the unknown that threatened us of what was to come. Beneath the tranquility lay an unspoken tension, a knowledge that our time together was fleeting. As I grew more attuned to my own voice, I also felt the weight of Melissa's burdens pressing down on her. I sensed the hurtfulness that surrounded her, an unshakeable shadow that lingered just out of sight... "Do you ever feel trapped by your own words, Melissa?" I asked her one night, my curiosity piqued by the complexity of her emotions, "Can poetry really set you free, or does it bind you to the mere words you express on the pages?"

Melissa considered the question I asked, her gaze distant, deep in thought, "Words can be both chains and wings, Maria Grace. They can tether us to our past, but they can also elevate us beyond it. The trick lies in knowing how to wield them. I've learned over the years to embrace the somberness, to use it as a means of expression, but it doesn't always come easily."

In those moments of honesty, I felt a deep respect for Melissa, and her untold struggles within. She had crafted a life filled with beauty and much despair, yet she remained suffocated, holding steadfast in her pursuit of a romantic meaning. I longed to understand her completely, to delve into the depths of her soul, but I knew that some secrets were meant to remain hidden, undiscovered, forever being a mystery.

As I look back now, I actually cherish those late evenings spent in the parlor of the brothel house, the faint laughter and the shared whispers drifting through the air like the scent of sweet incense. The poetry Melissa and I created became a tapestry of our experiences together, along with a mix of her unknown, painful past, a testament to our unorthodox connection amid the darkness that secretly surrounded us. Even after her absence, the verses we penned together continue to echo in my mind. They serve as a reminder, a cherished memory, of the tainted love we shared, the beauty that emerged from such pain, and the fragile bond that once illuminated our lives. In the heart of the French Quarter, where shadows linger around every corner, and memories intertwine, I hold onto these words of the past, this poetry, knowing they will forever be a part of me, a reflection of a lost friendship, a lost love, that shaped my immortal journey thus far.

Another tale comes to my mind that Melissa told me one night, as we practiced our poetry together...

'A dark romantic tale set in New Orleans... 'The last verse of Paul'... The French Quarter pulsed with life, its narrow streets soaked in history, mystery, and the rhythm of jazz music. Wrought-iron balconies sagged under the weight of creeping vines and various flowers, casting intricate shadows on cobbled alleys below, and the humid air of New Orleans seemed to hum with many secrets, secrets whispered in the stillness of the night, wrapped in the thick perfume of jasmine. It was here, in this labyrinth of mystic beauty and decay that Paul first saw her, Priscilla. She would become his muse, his obsession, and his ruin. Paul was not a man made for longevity, though his words could have outlived the ages. He was a poet by trade, a brooding artist with ink-stained fingers and a heart that harbored an endless well of melancholy. In the quiet corners of the French Quarter, Paul could often be found scrawling lines of verse, poetry, in notebooks worn thin with much use, sipping absinthe beneath the glow of antique lanterns. His work was admired but never famous, quietly appreciated by a few select patrons who saw the depth in his words, though perhaps not the darkness gnawing at the man himself. He was pale, gaunt, a man whose vitality seemed slowly leeching out like the colors of a fading photograph. But his eyes, blue as the twilight just after sunset, retained a fire that hinted at what once was, what could have been. It was at a poetry reading in a small, tucked-away cafe that he first laid eyes on her, Priscilla. She was radiant in the way that old myths speak of the women who would drive men to madness, dangerous, unknowable, and beautiful beyond reason. Her black hair, thick as night itself, cascaded down her slender back, framing her face with an ethereal glow beneath the candlelight. Paul's words faltered on his lips when she entered the room, for she was unlike anyone he had ever seen. There was something haunting about Priscilla, perhaps it was her smile, a smile that hinted at both amusement and a quiet sorrow, or perhaps it was the way she seemed to move through the world as though it were all temporary, like she was meant for something beyond it. Paul did not know then what drew him so irrevocably to her, only that he had no choice in the matter. His heart, fragile and frail as it was, had found its cage, and there was no escape. Paul approached her after his poetry reading, his hands trembling slightly as he clutched a copy of his chapbook. She was standing near the window, watching the world outside with an unreadable expression. The air between them felt electric as he crossed the floor, each step heavy with the weight of something unknown. "Miss Priscilla," Paul's voice wavered as he spoke, his heart beating so loudly that he was certain she could hear it. "I... I wanted to thank you for coming tonight. It means the world to me that someone like you would be here to listen."

Priscilla turned toward him, her lips curling into that same half-smile that had already begun to consume his thoughts, "Paul," she said softly, her voice smooth as silk, yet edged with something like sadness, "Your words... they are beautiful, very moving, but they are not complete."

Paul blinked, confused, "Not complete?"

"You write about love as though it's a distant dream," Priscilla replied, stepping closer, her eyes searching his face as though she could see beyond the surface. "But love isn't a dream, Paul. It's a storm, a fire, it's something that tears you apart and remakes you in its ashes."

Her words struck him deep, for they resonated with a truth he had always known but never dared to acknowledge. He had always written about love as though it were something to be admired from afar, too dangerous to touch. But here she was, Priscilla, speaking of love as though it were the very essence of destruction, and yet, he wanted it.

He wanted her, all of her. Days turned into weeks, and Paul found himself inextricably drawn into Priscilla's world. She was unlike any woman he had ever known, with a mind that danced between the realms of the living and the dead. Together, they wandered the French Quarter in the dead of night, the fog swirling around their feet like the restless spirits of the city itself. Paul's poetry changed; it became much darker, more visceral, as though Priscilla had unlocked a door in his soul that he had kept sealed for far too long. Their nights were filled with conversation and silence alike, both of which Paul found intoxicating. Priscilla would speak of death as though it were an old friend, as though she understood it in a way that no one else could. "Love and death," she would say, her voice a whisper in the shadows, "they are two sides of the same nature. To love is to court death, Paul."

He would listen, rapt, even as something inside him ached with the knowledge that he was losing himself to her. There were moments when he could feel his illness clawing at him, his breath shallow, his heart weak, but he never told her. He couldn't. To speak of his sickness would be to shatter the illusion of invincibility she had woven around him. He wanted only to be strong for her, to be the man she deserved, even as he knew his time was running short, he could feel it within his bones. As the weeks passed, Paul's health deteriorated, though he hid it well. Priscilla would notice the occasional cough, the pallor in his skin, the scent easing from inside his body, but she never pressed him on it. Perhaps, she already knew, perhaps she understood that something was wrong, but in her own way, she allowed him his silence. Their relationship grew to love, with their love becoming a tempest, a thing of beauty and terror, as Paul threw himself into the fire with no thought of escape, but every moment of passion, every stolen kiss in the darkened streets, Paul could feel the end creeping closer. His body was failing him, the sickness growing stronger with each passing day.

The doctors had warned him many months ago, there was nothing they could do, only time would tell how long he had left. But he made his choice, he would not tell Priscilla. He would not let her bear the weight of his dying. One balmy October evening, Paul and Priscilla found themselves walking by the Mississippi River. The moon hung low in the sky, casting a silver glow on the water's surface. Paul's breath came in shallow gasps, though he masked it as best he could. He wanted this night to last forever. He wanted to freeze this moment in time, to hold onto it before everything slipped away. "Do you believe in fate, Paul?" Priscilla asked suddenly, breaking the quiet. She was staring out at the river, her eyes distant.

Paul blinked, startled by the question, "I don't know," he admitted. "I've always thought that we make our own destiny, free to weave our own path by the choices we make, but since meeting you... I am not so sure now."

She turned to him, her gaze piercing through the fog that seemed to settle between them. "I think we were always meant to meet, you and I," Priscilla said softly. "But I do not think we're meant to last."

The words struck Paul like a physical blow, and for a moment, he could not breathe. "What do you mean?" he replied, though deep down, he already knew.

"There's something in your eyes," Priscilla murmured, stepping closer to him, "Something broken. You've been dying since the moment I met you, haven't you?"

Paul felt the weight of her words settle on him like a shroud. He wanted to deny it, to push the truth away, but he could not. Not anymore. His chest tightened, and for a moment, he thought he might collapse right there by the riverbank, but instead, he reached for her, pulling her into his arms. "I didn't want you to know any of this yet," Paul said hoarsely, "I didn't want to burden you with this."

Priscilla's eyes filled with something that looked like grief, though she did not cry. "You think you're sparing me, but you are not," she whispered. "You've been dying in front of me this whole time, and I couldn't stop it."

"I think I love you, Priscilla," Paul's blurted out, his voice breaking, "I love you."

She smiled sadly, her cold fingers tracing the line of his jaw, "I know, Paul," she replied. "But love can't save you, not this time."

The night stretched on, and they stayed by the river until the first light of dawn began to creep over the horizon. Paul felt weaker than ever, his limbs heavy, his breath shallow, and his body exhausted. Priscilla remained by his side, silent and still, as though she were waiting for something. It was on that riverbank, as the sun began to rise, that Paul finally succumbed to the sickness that had been ravaging his body for so long. His final breath was taken in Priscilla's arms, his last sight was the soft glow of the morning light on her angelic, darkness-filled face, and in that moment, as death wrapped its cold arms around him, Paul felt a strange sense of peace. He had truly loved Priscilla, he had lived, if only for a brief, burning moment, he knew what true love felt like. Priscilla did not weep. She only held him until the sun had fully risen, her face unreadable. Then, slowly, she rose to her feet as she placed Paul's lifeless body onto the moist ground and looked out over the river one last time before walking away, leaving him behind, leaving a love, a great man, an exceptional poet, behind. In the weeks that followed, the French Quarter continued its eternal dance of life and death, its secrets hidden beneath layers of time, and in the quiet corners of the city, people spoke in faint whispers of the poet who had loved too deeply, who had written of death without ever truly understanding it until the end. But Priscilla was never seen again. Some say that she left the city, unable to bear the weight of her loss, while others say she had been a ghost, an angel, or an immortal, just a specter haunting the streets of New Orleans, waiting for a love that could never last. Whatever the truth, one thing remained clear, Paul's final verses, his dark poetry, would live on, carried by the wind through the narrow alleys and along the riverbanks of a city that had witnessed countless stories of love and loss. For Paul, love had been both his salvation and his destruction, and in the end, it had been the last thing he had ever wrote about...

'For Priscilla'

In shadows deep where moonlight fades,

I found you waiting, cloaked in shades,

A dream, a whisper, dark and sweet,

A love too fierce for time to keep.

Your eyes, a storm, your touch, a flame,

I burned, yet never spoke your name,

For hearts like ours are bound to fall,

To love is death, it's worth it all,

So, take this breath, my final plea,

In you, my love, my eternity.

The echoes of Paul's last, final words lingered in the moist air of the French Quarter, a poetic epitaph to a life lived in the shadow of both love and death. In those winding streets, amid the flowers and fog, his story would remain etched in the hearts of those who had known him, a testament to the truth that love, though fleeting, can leave a mark deeper than eternity itself.'

Melissa's tales often struck my heart, but this story that she told me that night, was by far the deepest, it was actually one of my favorite tales that she spoke of. Although, I'm not sure why it struck my heart so deeply, I have always cherished its meaning, its sadness. My mind ponders often, thinking if any of these stories were of any type of truth, if they were Melissa's hidden confessions of her past.

Chapter 6

As I continue to gaze out the window of the hotel that once served as a brothel house, the bustling streets of New Orleans unfold before me, vibrant and alive. The French Quarter full of tourists with sounds of mingled laughter and chatter, distant sounds of jazz music, a melody that wraps around the city like a warm embrace. Yet, as I dwell in this sanctuary of the hotel, memories, I can't help but reflect on the transformation that has taken place within these hotel walls, a metamorphosis that mirrors my own journey through the ages.

The brothel house had once been the only refuge I'd known, a refuge for lost souls, a place where one could come to find employment, a hot meal, or just a place to rest one's head. It thrived in an era when secrecy was currency, and the allure of the forbidden was woven into the very fabric of the French Quarter. I remember the dimly lit corridors, the hallways, the conversations faintly heard, that echoed through the private rooms, and the whispers of silk against skin. It was a world filled with much passion and desire, but some with heartache, a place where I learned both joys and sorrows could collide.

As the years passed, societal norms shifted, and the world began to frown upon the very establishments that had once flourished. The brothel's allure waned, overshadowed by the rise of new morals and expectations, with each passing decade, the shadows grew heavier, and I knew that I needed to adapt, to reinvent myself in a world that demanded change. In the quiet of the night, I made the decision that would alter the course of my adaptation. I would transform my brothel house into a fine hotel, a haven for weary travelers seeking solace in the heart of the city. It was a clever disguise, allowing me to retain the history of these ancient walls while embracing the modern era. As I walked through these familiar halls, I envisioned brighter rooms filled with more sunlight, even though, I would never get to witness the sun beaming through the windows of these decorative rooms, plush bedding, and the gentle hum of innocent laughter replacing the whispers of desire.

The transition was not without its challenges. I poured my heart and undead soul into the intense renovations, determined to maintain the same essence of what had come before while ushering in a new era. I selected vibrant colors that reflected the rich culture of New Orleans, deep blues, warm golds, and vibrant greens, and adorned the walls with artwork that spoke the city's spirit. Each room became a tribute to the lives once lived here, a blend of elegance and history that would draw guests from far and wide. Within this historical landmark in the heart of the French Quarter, still remained the parlor, where I shared so many nights with Melissa, the parlor was the only piece of the place, a once vibrant brothel, that was left the same. I did not alter its design, I let it remain in its original form, along with all my memories of Melissa.

Yet beneath the surface of my new endeavors lay the ever-present reality of my existence as an immortal, a vampire. I had to navigate the delicate balance between maintaining my wealth and preserving the secrecy of my true nature. The hotel flourished, drawing in patrons who sought the charm of the French Quarter, while I remained hidden in the shadows as a vampire lurking beneath the surface. After a while, the myths about vampires became entertainment, that's when I began to mingle and surface more during the night hours. I would mingle with various guests, speaking to them and listening to where they came from and so on. They would just assume I was a part of the festivities and festive costume parties that reside throughout the Quarter on a regular basis now. Casually, when the blood hunger was unbearable, I often found myself slipping into the night, cloaked in darkness as I roamed the crowded streets, intertwining with the living, the many tourists that flooded Bourbon Street. The vibrant energy that, now, embraced this city was sometimes intoxicating, a stark contrast to the solitude I once felt. I watch the visitors, as well as the local residents, wander along the streets of the Quarter, and the ones who enter my hotel, their faces alight with excitement and curiosity, unaware of the history that surrounds them. It was a bittersweet experience to adjust to this new culture, with all my past memories still echoing in the hallways, a faint reminder of the life I had chosen, even if it was against my will, a life filled with shadows and buried secrets.

As I settled into my nightly role as a hotelier, I began to cultivate discreet relationships with my employees, the ones hired to maintain the functioning of the hotel, especially through the daylight hours. Without their knowledge, my staff became my eyes and ears in the world, each of them unaware of the depths of my past, my true nature. I chose individuals who resonated with the spirit of the French Quarter, who knew some of the history about my hotel, when it was once a brothel house, individuals who have heard faint stories of the mystery to the place. Artists, musicians, and dreamers, hoping to keep the essence, the history, of the long-ago brothel house alive in its new form. My workers breathe life into my hotel, infusing it with much creativity and passion, and I found solace in their silly chatters and camaraderie.

Despite the full transformation of the hotel, I still felt the heaviness of my past, my history, pressing down on me, as the echoes of Melissa's laughter, her whispers, the shadows of our shared past, still lingered in the air, reminding me of the choices made, and who I really was. There were nights when I would sit alone in the parlor, tracing my finger over the restored furniture, the velvet chairs, that had once cradled our many conversations. I would read the poems we had written together, allowing the words to wash over me like a balm for my restless soul. In these quiet moments, I often reflected on the mere price of immortality, I had crafted a type of life filled with beauty, luxury, yet it was accompanied by an undercurrent of past sorrows. The hotel became a refuge for others, but for me, it was my eternal prison. I knew I could never leave this dwelling. This place served as a constant reminder of the love, the loss, that will forever shape me. The memories held within this hotel, this once vibrant brothel, will always linger, intertwined with the joys of the present, a picture of what had brought me to this point in my undead life.

I remembered a tale told to me, by Melissa, during one of our late-night conversations...

'It was the early 1500's in Paris, a city where history was written in stone and blood. The Seine wound its way through the heart of this medieval metropolis like a vein of life, its waters flowing steadily, oblivious to the stories etched into the very walls of the city. Yet amidst the everyday hustle of merchants and artists, there was one who walked the narrow, winding streets unnoticed. She moved with the elegance of a faint shadow, her steps silent as the night itself. Elisabeth had been many things over the centuries: a noblewoman, a hunter, a seeker of forgotten knowledge, but above all, she had been lonely. Immortality had proven to be a cruel gift, offering her endless years of life but no solace for her heart. A vampire, cursed to live in mere darkness, she had watched lovers come and go, friendships bloom and wither, but none could stand the test of time as she did. None could share in her eternal existence without fear. Her alabaster skin, unmarked by the passing of centuries, her long raven-like hair flowing freely behind her like a cascade of midnight, and her piercing emerald eyes made her a vision of pure, dark beauty that could stop men in their tracks, but beneath that fine surface lay a torment no mortal, no human, could ever comprehend. Elisabeth's heart was as cold as her freezing skin, frozen by the curse that bound her to the night, and yet, despite her centuries of existence, one desire had never died, the desire for love. She had long ceased to hope for someone who would truly understand her suffering, who would share her endless night, and who could be strong enough to remain with her for eternity. Still, the aching void inside her undead heart would not be silenced, and so, she roamed, seeking, yearning, with an undying heart full of sorrow and such longing.

The night was cool and damp as Elisabeth wandered the dirty streets of Paris, her senses heightened by the hunger for blood gnawing at her from within. She had not fed in several nights, resisting the temptation that threatened to overtake her at every turn. The scent of human blood was everywhere, thick in the air as people shuffled about, unaware of the predator lurking among them. She could hear the heartbeats of the passerby, could smell the faint hint of life in their skin, but still she resisted. The hunger, the guilt every time she fed was brutal, but she had learned, this hunger could be controlled, at least for a while. Even though, it was always just as hard to resist. Paris in the early 1500's was a city of contradictions, the grandeur of Notre-Dame loomed in the distance, its towers rising high against the darkened sky, a symbol of human aspiration and devotion. But in the shadows of its mighty spires, the streets were filled with many beggars, thieves, and lost souls. Elisabeth had seen it all unfold, had watched as the city shifted and changed, but one thing had remained constant, her isolation. She moved through the crowd, unnoticed as always, her eyes scanning the faces around her. She searched for something she had not yet found in all her immortal years, someone who might actually see her, truly see her, for what she was. But the fear of rejection weighed heavily on her undead heart. No human could ever accept the monster that she had become, not without fear or revulsion, and yet, her heart, still clinging to the last shreds of its humanity, refused to give up the search. It was on a quiet side street, away from the bustle of the markets and the taverns, that she first saw him. He stood under a flickering streetlamp, his back turned to her, but even from a distance, Elisabeth could sense something different about him. He was tall, with dark, unruly hair and an aura of melancholy that seemed to mirror her own. There was a stillness to him, a quietness that drew her in, and before she realized it, her feet were moving toward him, as though some unseen force had taken hold of her, as if she was mere floating in the air. Her undead heart, which had not beat for centuries, quickened with anticipation. Could this be the one? Could this be the very soul that would finally understand her loneliness? The thought was absurd, she knew, and yet she couldn't stop herself from hoping still. As she approached, he turned. Their eyes met, and for the first time in centuries, Elisabeth felt a spark of something she had thought long dead. His eyes were a deep, stormy blue, filled with a sadness that mirrored her own. In that moment, the world around them seemed to fall away, and for the first time in almost forever, she did not feel entirely alone.

His name was Lucien, and like Elisabeth, he too had known loss. He had come to Paris seeking solace after the death of his beloved, a woman he had cherished more than life itself. He spoke of her often, his voice heavy with much grief, and Elisabeth found herself drawn to his sadness. It was a pain she understood all too well. Night after night, Elisabeth and Lucien would meet under the same streetlamp, talking until the first light of dawn threatened to chase her away. Lucien was a dark poet, his words laced with a sorrow that reflected her own. They spoke of love, of loss, of the cruel passage of time, and slowly, Elisabeth began to feel something stir within her immortal body, something she hadn't felt in many, many years. Elisabeth allowed herself to hope, perhaps Lucien could be the one man to fill the eternal void that had gnawed at her for so long. Perhaps, just perhaps, she could love again, but deep down, she knew the cold truth, she could never offer him the life he truly deserved. She was a creature of the night, cursed to always live in the darkness, and no matter how much she longed to be with Lucien, she knew that her nature would always stand in the way.

Despite her better judgement, Elisabeth found herself falling for Lucien. His gentle words, his quiet strength, and the way he seemed to truly see her, beyond the monster she had become; it was more than she had ever hoped for, but with each passing night, the blood hunger inside her grew more insistent. She had not fed in weeks, and it was becoming harder and harder to resist the evil temptation that Lucien's very presence stirred within her. She had sworn to herself that she would never harm him, unlike all the others she loved in the past, that she would not let the inner beast in her ruin the one thing that had brought her a little happiness in centuries, but the hunger was getting relentless, and with every passing night, she felt her control slipping away.

Lucien, oblivious to the danger he was in, continued to meet Elisabeth night after night. He found himself drawn to her in a way that he could not explain. There was something mysterious about her, something dark and mystic, that called to him. She was unlike any woman he had ever known, beautiful, yes, but there was something more. There was sadness, deep sorrow, in her hollow eyes that he recognized, a loneliness that echoed his own. He never imagined he could ever love someone again, but now, after meeting Elisabeth, it might actually be possible. One night, as they stood by the Seine, Lucien reached for her hand. Elisabeth flinched at the warm touch, pulling away before he could feel the mere coldness of her skin, but Lucien was not deterred. "Elisabeth," he said, his voice soft in the darkness of the moonlit night, "why do you push me away?"

Elisabeth looked at him, her unbeaten heart aching with the weight of the truth that she could never tell him. How could she explain the evil monster that lurked within her? How could she tell him that she had lived for many centuries, feeding on the blood of the innocent and no so innocent mortal beings, cursed to walk this earth alone for all eternity? "I cannot give you what you desire, Lucien," she said, her voice barely more than a whisper, "I am not what you think me to be."

Lucien frowned, his eyes searching hers for answers, "I don't care what you are, Elisabeth. I care about who you are, and I know that there is something more to you than this sadness you seem to carry."

Elisabeth turned away, her heart heavy by the words he just spoke. How could she make him understand? How could she tell him the real truth without losing him forever? "I cannot," she mumbled, her voice trembling, "I cannot love you, Lucien. Not in the way that you want me to."

Even as she said the words, she knew they were a lie, she did love him, and could love him in the way he desired, but he would not truly understand her nature and he would flee in fear, like the others in the past, and she would just have to end his existence, just as in the past. She had loved him from the moment she had laid eyes on him, but her love was a dangerous thing, a dark and twisted thing that could only bring pain and suffering. Lucien stepped closer, his hands gracefully touching her chilled cheek, "Then let me love you, Elisabeth. Let me be the one to take your sadness, your loneliness, away."

For a brief moment, Elisabeth allowed herself to believe that it could actually work, that they could find happiness together, but the blood hunger inside her was growing stronger by the minute, and she knew that it was only a matter of time before she lost control of it. She stepped back quickly, breaking the intimate connection between them, "I cannot!" she repeated her words, her voice stronger this time, "You just don't understand!"

It was on a stormy night, when the rain poured down in heavy sheets and the streets of Paris were deserted, that Elisabeth's world came crashing down. She had avoided Lucien for several nights, knowing that her blood hunger control was slipping, that the creature within her was becoming harder to tame, but she could not stay away from him forever. Lucien finally found her by the river, where they had spent so many nights together. His face was pale, his eyes filled with a mixture of confusion and slight fear, "Elisabeth," he said, his voice nervous, "I know."

Elisabeth's unbeaten heart seemed to stop all over again, "What do you know, Lucien?"

"I told you before, I've seen you," he murmured, "I've seen what, and who, you really are."

The world seemed to tilt beneath her feet, he knew. He knew what she was. The one thing she had feared most had come to pass, and now there was no going back. She really did not want to lose him or have to end his existence. "I saw you," Lucien continued, his voice barely hearable over the sound of the rain. "I saw you feed on someone."

Elisabeth's immortal blood seemed to run cold. She had been careful, so careful. She couldn't contain her hunger any longer and had to go out and take a life, but somehow, he had seen her in the act, had witnessed the evil creature, the monster, she truly was. Interrupting her inner thought, "I don't care," Lucien said, stepping closer with determined, nervous confidence. "I do not care what you really are, Elisabeth, I love you, whether you are evil or not."

His words pierced her undead heart like a dagger. He loved her, even after seeing the darkness that lurked within her, he loved her, but she knew that love was not enough. It would never be enough. "You just cannot understand," Elisabeth whispered, her voice broken, as a blood tear rolled down her cool cheek, "I am immortal, Lucien. I cannot love you without the fear of destroying you."

Lucien shook his head, his eyes filled with much desperation, "Then, you will just have to take that chance, destroy me if it is necessary," he said, his voice rising with emotion, "I would rather be destroyed by you than live without you."

Elisabeth could feel the hunger rising deep within her, as she caught a whiff of Lucien's blood cross her nostrils. She could feel the inner beast, the inner demon, clawing its way to the surface. She had fought it for so long, it seemed, the tempting need to taste Lucien's sweet-smelling blood, had resisted its pull, but now, standing in front of him, the man she loved, she knew she could not fight it any longer. "I can't," she mumbled, blood tears streaming slowly down her face, "I can't do this."

Lucien, unaware of her struggle within, stepped closer, his arms wrapping around her in a desperate embrace, "I love you, Elisabeth," he said, his lips brushing against her cold ear, "I really do love you, and nothing will ever change that."

The blood hunger roared within her, louder than it had ever been before. She could feel her fangs lengthening, could feel the darkness overtaking her, and in that moment, she knew what she had to do. With a cry of anguish, she pushed him away, her body shaking with the effort of holding back the evil fate this outraged hunger could unleash. "Go," she stated, her voice hoarse with emotion, "Go, before it's too late for you, Lucien."

But Lucien did not move. He stood there, firm, his eyes locked on hers, his love for her shining through the darkness, "I'm not leaving you." he said, boldly with his voice steady, brave.

Elisabeth could feel the last of her control losing its grip, she could not fight it any longer. His blood scent was just too strong. With a scream of despair, she lunged at Lucien, her fangs sinking deep into his neck. The taste of his blood filled her mouth, and for a moment, this blood hunger was sated. As she drank his blood, she realized what she had done. She pulled away, horror flooding her as she felt the amazing sensation of his blood course through her body. She looked down at Lucien's lifeless body, she had killed him. The one person who had truly loved her despite the dark creature she was, the one person who had made her feel alive again, was gone.

Elisabeth stood by the river, the rain still pouring down around her. The city of Paris stretched out before her, indifferent to her pain, just as it had been indifferent to the centuries of loneliness she had endured. She had loved, and in doing so, she had destroyed the only thing that had ever mattered to her. As the rain ceased to fall, after Lucien's life was taken, Elisabeth found a small piece of paper in his fist, crumbled, but readable...

'To My Dark Beloved'
I loved you in the shadows deep,
Where light and hope no longer creep,
Your eyes, a mirror to the night,
A beauty born of endless blight.
I kissed your lips of ice and stone,
But knew the grave would take its own,
For in your arms, I felt the cold,
The ache of centuries untold.
Still, I would give my fleeting breath,
To taste your love, though bound by death,
For even if I fade to dust,
My soul will find you, as it must.
In darkness, we are meant to part,
Yet you remain, my broken heart.

For centuries to come Elisabeth would wander the dark streets of Paris, haunted by the memory of the man who had really loved her, who did not fear her. She would search for him in the face of strangers, but she would never find him. The love she had sought for so long had slipped through her fingers, and now she was truly alone in her own cruel madness of her immortal mind. The blood hunger, the darkness, the curse of immortality, they would be her only companions from now on, and as the years passed, she would come to understand that the true curse of immortality was not the endless years of life, but the endless grief of losing the one she loved, the one taken by her own greediness, by the mere lust of human blood. And so, Elisabeth, the vampire who had loved and lost, would forever roam the dirty streets of Paris during the late nights for all eternity, a shadow among shadows, always seeking, searching, for a love that could never really be hers.'

Coming back to my reality, as I still linger at my window, I ponder on Melissa's tale. The mere sadness of it still consumes my undead heart even now. Yet, as the moon rises high over the rooftops of the French Quarter, I knew I had carved out a space for myself here, a sanctuary where I could exist in both my worlds. The hotel, a symbol of my resilience, stood as a testament to my ability to adapt, to rise from the ashes of my past while holding onto the memories that defined me. And so, I will continue to embrace the paradox of my mere existence, weaving together the threads of love, loss, and rebirth as I drift through the delicate dance between the living and the dead. In the heart of this French Quarter of New Orleans, where shadows and light collide, I found a semblance of peace, though faint, it's still a small sanctuary where the echoes of my unforgotten past could coexist with the vibrancy of the present.

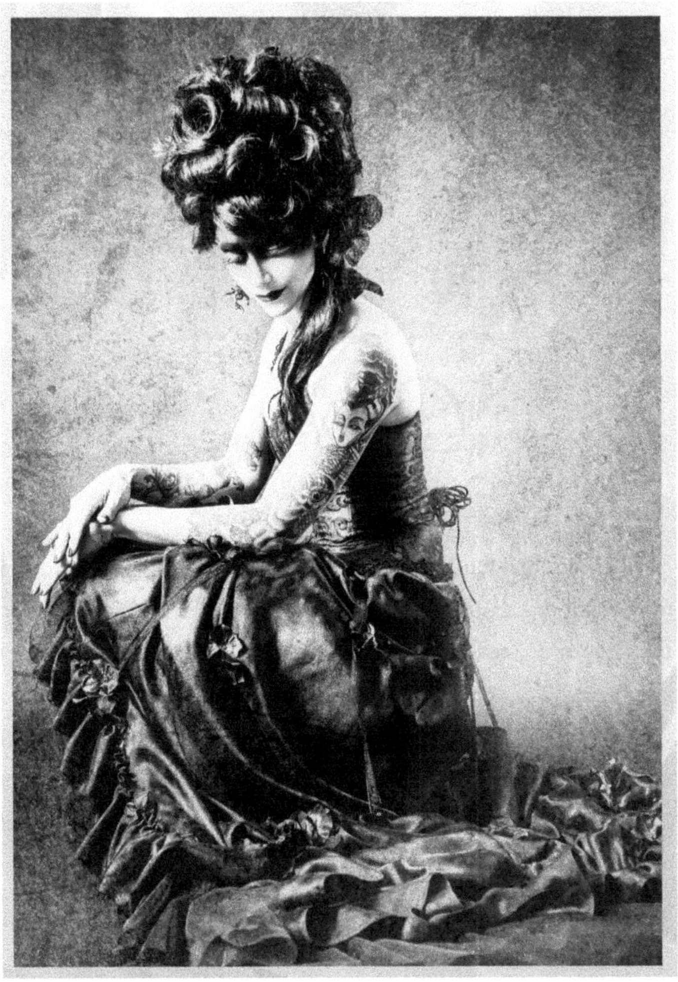

Chapter 7

As the moonlight continued to filter through the lace curtains of my hotel room, casting delicate patterns on the hardwood floor, my thoughts turned to my only true love, Patrick, the man who had swept into my life like a summer breeze and vanished just as quickly, leaving a void that I would never try to fill again. I still remembered the way his sandy-blonde hair caught the sunlight, the glint of seductive mischief in his green eyes that always seemed to promise adventure. Our brief moments together had been electric, yet the love we shared felt like a candle flickering in the wind, against the vastness of a cold night.

In the back of my mind, a story Melissa once told me echoed over my thoughts of Patrick, a tale of star-crossed lovers doomed by fate. She had painted a picture of passion and much loss, her voice, as I remembered, tinged with both nostalgia and sadness... "In another time," she had said, "there was a couple, two souls, destined to be together but torn apart by forces beyond their control. They loved deeply, yet the universe conspired against them...

'In 1597, New Orleans was still an unformed dream, a city rising from the marshy bayou lands, its future veiled in mystery. The air was suffocating, thick with humidity, and the scent of cypress trees and brackish water clung to the wind. At night, the city whispered ancient secrets, a place where the boundaries between the living and the dead, the natural and the supernatural, were as thin as the Spanish moss hanging from the old oak trees. The French Quarter, with its narrow streets and hidden courtyards, was already a place where magic pulsed beneath the surface. It attracted all sorts: adventurers, traders, mystics, and those seeking a life beyond the rigid boundaries of the Old World. Here, fate and destiny held their own kind of power, and in the heart of this burgeoning city, two souls, Matthew and Victoria, were bound by a love so deep, so consuming, that even the universe itself would conspire to tear them apart.

Matthew had always been a man marked by darkness. He came from an old Creole family, his lineage entangled with the mysteries of the land. His mother, known for her knowledge of herbs and the whispers of the unseen, had raised him with stories of spirits, curses, and omens, but despite his connection to the supernatural, Matthew carried an air of melancholy, a loneliness that had settled deep within him like a shadow. At twenty-nine, he had inherited the family trade of shipping, working along the Mississippi River, where he spent his days moving goods for New Orleans' growing population. He preferred the night, though, when the city fell into a hushed quiet, and the dark waters of the river seemed to mirror the sky. It was during one of those nights that he first saw her, Victoria.

Victoria was unlike anyone Matthew had ever seen. She moved through the streets of the Quarter with a grace that was almost ethereal, her long, raven-black hair flowing down her back, her skin pale as moonlight against the backdrop of the humid night, her eyes, deep and dark, seemed to hold many secrets older than the city itself. She wore a gown of deep indigo, the fabric trailing behind her like the night sky, dotted with the glitter of stars. She was the daughter of a powerful French merchant, her family well known among the high society of New Orleans, though Victoria herself always seemed apart from the world she inhabited. She was destined to marry one of her father's business partners, a cruel man who sought power and wealth above all else.

The moment Matthew saw her, the world around him seemed to fade, as if time itself had paused to allow their meeting. He stood on the corner of Royal Street, watching her from the shadows, almost like a mere stalker. When their eyes finally met, something shifted in the stale air, as though an invisible force had drawn their souls together. Neither spoke, but something passed between them, a recognition, as if they had known each other in another life, another time. It was merely like 'love' at first sight. Victoria stopped, her gaze lingering on Matthew. Her lips parted, but no words came. Instead, she simply nodded a shy nod, an acknowledgement of the connection that now seemed to bound them, and then, just as quickly, she disappeared into the night, leaving Matthew standing there, breathless and changed.

From that night on, Matthew and Victoria found themselves drawn to each other, meeting in secret beneath the shroud of darkness. The world around them seemed to dissolve when they were together, embraced, the weight of their lives, their obligations, forgotten in the soft whispers of their secret love. They met in hidden courtyards, away from the prying eyes of Victoria's father and the man she was betrothed to, a cruel plantation owner named Renault. He was a man of immense power and riches, known for his ruthless dealings and his hunger for control. He cared very little for Victoria's happiness; to him, she was a prize, a means to secure greater influence. But in those sacred moments, Matthew and Victoria found such solace. They would sit by the river, watching the reflection of the moon ripple across the water, or walk through the thick, fog-shrouded streets of the French Quarter, lost in the intensity of their passion, yet, from the beginning, they knew their love was doomed, impossible to have. There were forces at play that neither could fully understand, forces older than New Orleans itself, woven into the very fabric of the land. Victoria's family was deeply involved in old-world politics, and her father had made dark pacts with influential men to secure his position in the colony. Matthew, though he tried to hide it, carried a dark legacy of his own, a curse passed down through his Creole family that marked him as different. His mother had warned him, ever since he was a young child, that their family bloodline was cursed. They were tied to the spirits of the bayou, bound to the will of forces that could not be seen or touched. Matthew had never really believed her stories, but the more time he spent with Victoria, the more he felt the weight of something tragic, unseen pressing down on him.

One night, as Matthew and Victoria sat beneath the shadow of a large oak tree, the Spanish moss draping over them like a curtain, Victoria turned to Matthew with warm tears in her eyes. "We cannot go on like this, Matthew," she whispered, her voice trembling, "My father will never let us be together, to build any kind of future, and Renault... he's a dangerous man. If he finds out about us, he will kill you."

Matthew took her fragile hands in his, his heart heavy with the weight of her words, "I don't care what they say, Victoria. I won't lose you, not to them."

Tears slipped down her pale cheeks, "But there's more... something else. There's something... something dark that follows us, Matthew. I can't explain it, but I can feel it, ever since we met. It has been there, lurking over us in the shadows. It's like... like the universe itself does not want us to be together."

Matthew felt it too. The sense of being watched, of something unseen moving just beyond the edge of their perception. The air around them always seemed to grow colder when they were together, the shadows deeper, but he refused to believe that their love was just a mistake, forbidden to be. As their love, their relationship grew, deepened, so did the unseen forces that worked against them. Victoria's father, Armand, was not a man to be crossed. He had built his fortune on blood and deceit, making deals with men as ruthless as Renault and others even more dangerous. Unknown to Victoria, her father was also tied to the darker side of New Orleans, the secret world of voodoo and ancient rites that thrived beneath the surface of the city. He had made pacts, promises by blood, with powerful practitioners, promising his daughter to Renault in exchange for protection and prosperity, mere power and riches. Renault, too, was no ordinary man. He dabbled in dark magic, using his wealth and influences to control not only the living but also the dark spirits of the dead. It was rumored that he had the power to summon the loa, the spirits of the voodoo pantheon, and bend them to his own will, and he was well aware of Victoria's affair with Matthew.

One night, while Victoria and Matthew met in secret at the edge of the swampy bayou, Renault made his move. With the help of a voodoo priestess, he cast a binding spell, trapping Matthew's spirit in a web of dark magic. The curse was very ancient, designed to separate soulmates, to keep them apart for eternity. Victoria felt the dark change immediately. She had been waiting for Matthew by the bayou when a chilling, cold wind swept through the trees, the night suddenly growing still and oppressive. The familiar warmth of Matthew's presence was gone, replaced by an overwhelming sense of dark dread. Panic gripped her heart as she searched for him, calling his name into the utter darkness, but Matthew was nowhere to be found. It was as if he had simply vanished from the world, his very essence pulled from reality.

Days turned into weeks, and still, there was no sign of Matthew. Victoria was consumed by much sadness, much grief, her once vibrant spirit withering under the weight of Matthew's absence. She refused to believe that he was really gone forever, certain that something much darker, evil, was to blame. Desperate to find some answers, Victoria turned to the only source she could think of, the voodoo priestess, Marie Laveau, a powerful woman who was said to have much knowledge of the spirit world. Marie Laveau had lived in the Quarter for many years, her reputation both feared and respected. She was known for her ability to commune with the dead and bend the will of the spirits to her command. When Victoria arrived at Marie's small, dimly lit cabin deep in the bayou, the priestess seemed to be expecting her. The air inside the cabin was thick with the smell of much incense and dried herbs hanging all over the ceiling, and the flickering of several candles cast long, eerie shadows on the walls. "You seek the one who is lost," Marie said before Victoria could even speak.

Victoria nodded, her voice nervous with slight fear, "My Matthew... he's gone. I do not know what happened to him, but I can feel him. He's still out there somewhere."

Marie Laveau studied her for a long moment, her dark eyes unreadable, "The one you seek, the one you love has been taken by dark magic, magic you cannot comprehend, girl. His soul is bound, trapped between worlds of darkness."

Victoria's heart raced, "Can you bring him back? Can you save him?"

Marie shook her head, "It's not that simple, girl. Very dark magic has been placed upon him, dark magic that has been marked and used to separate you both, magic older than this land itself, girl. To undo it would require a sacrifice, one that could cost you your very soul."

Victoria did not care, she would do anything to save Matthew, to be with him again, even if it meant facing the darkness itself. Marie Laveau led Victoria through the darkness of the bayou, to a place where the veil between worlds was thin, a place where the dead and the living could meet. Under the light of a full moon, Marie began the sacred, forbidden ritual, calling upon the loa to guide Matthew's spirit back to the world of the living, but as the ritual progressed, something went badly wrong. The air grew heavier, and the once peaceful night turned violent, with strong winds howling through the trees. Dark shapes moved in the creepy shadows, the spirits that Renault had summoned to keep Matthew trapped was fighting back against Marie's magic. Victoria could feel Matthew's presence, but it was faint, as if he were calling to her from a great distance. She could see him, but he was faraway and almost ghostly. She reached out, her heart aching with the effort, desperate to pull him back to her. But in that moment, a choice was placed before her. Marie Laveau's voice, low and filled with urgency, cut through the chaos, "You must decide, girl. To bring him back, you must offer your soul in his place. Are you willing to pay this price?"

Victoria did not hesitate, "Yes. Whatever it takes, I will do it. Just bring him back!"

Marie nodded grimly and completed the ritual, binding Victoria's soul to the darkness in exchange for Matthew's return.

Matthew did return, but not as he once was. He had been changed by the dark magic that had trapped him, his once warm and loving nature, now cold and distant. Victoria, too, had been altered. Though her sacrifice had brought him back, her soul had been marked by the evil darkness she had embraced. They were together again, but their love was no longer the pure, consuming force it had once been. Instead, it was tainted, weighed down by the price they had both had to pay. In the end, the universe had conspired to tear them apart, and even though they had fought against it, they had truly lost. Their love, once destined to transcend time and space, had been broken by darkness, by dark magic, beyond their control. And so, they remained in New Orleans, haunted by the echoes of what they once had, their souls bound together yet forever torn apart. It was merely a love that wasn't meant to be.'

This small tale made my mind twist back to that dreadful night... It was during one of those late-night storytelling sessions, with the air heavy with incense and the storm raging outside as the lightning bolted across the dark skies, that I first felt the sting of understanding, of what it meant to love fiercely yet face inevitable loss. I could plainly see Patrick's face in that story, the bright spark of our connection mirrored in the tragic fates of those fictional lovers, that Melissa spoke of, but nothing compared to the raw pain I felt the night Patrick disappeared from me forever. That day had started with much inspiration, I was to leave with my finance at noon, when he would be arriving with the carriage that would take us far from the brothel house and Melissa, yet he never showed. The carriage never came, and Patrick was never to be heard of again. All the shared dreams, secrets told to each other, and the plans for a future together, now felt like a cruel illusion, as the sun hung proud that day, warming my skin as I waited impatiently in front of the brothel house in the French Quarter. Then, just as quickly as all these hopes began, it was all over. I can still recall the chill that gripped my heart when Melissa summoned me to her room, later that night. Her emerald eyes, usually so vibrant, were clouded with a shadow I had never witnessed before, "Maria Grace, my dear," she said, her voice softer than the rustle of silk, "Patrick is gone. He... He will not be returning."

Despair flooded my senses, an ocean of grief crashing over me as I sank to the floor, my heart shattering, "What do you mean? He just left. He wouldn't... He wouldn't abandon me like that!" My voice trembled in fury, disbelief twisting through my chest like a vine strangling a delicate flower.

Melissa knelt beside me, pulling me into her embrace, her cool skin against mine, a stark reminder of the world I inhabited now, "Sometimes, the threads of fate are beyond our control," she murmured, stroking my hair, "He loved you, Maria Grace, but there are forces in this world that we cannot understand."

In that exact moment, I hated her for her cryptic words, yet I needed her comfort more than ever. Melissa held me tight, her presence a medicine to my shattered heart, but I could not escape the reality of my loss. It was a tragedy woven into my very being, an ache that would haunt me for centuries to come.

Later, as a means of solace, Melissa gifted me with a vintage silver mirror, a hand-held piece that shimmered under the candlelight. It felt heavy in my palms, both a burden and a treasure. The ornate frame was etched with intricate designs, like twisting vines that seemed to come alive under my fingertips. I gracefully traced the patterns absentmindedly, mesmerized by the way it captured not just my reflection but the essence of my sorrow.

"Keep this close, Maria Grace," she said, with her voice soft, comforting yet commanding with a serious tone, "It holds memories of the past and glimpses of the future. It is a reminder of you who are, who you will always be. Legend says this looking-glass, this mirror, is special. It's the only mirror that exists, where an immortal, a vampire, can actually see their reflection."

Winking a small wink at me, Melissa kissed the top of my head with her frozen lips, I giggled at her last words as I looked into the mirror. I realize now that she was being truthful about this mirror. Seeing my reflection in the glass, I saw not just my youthful face but the echoes of a life almost foreign. Fragments of my childhood flickered in and out of focus, my mother's warm embrace, the scent of lavender that always filled our home. I slowly remembered my mother sitting in the garden, crafting wishes on delicate pieces of paper, her smile swirling through the air as she burned them in the flame of the small fire, urging the smoke to carry them high into the sky, to carry her dreams beyond the universe, "Every wish holds the power, sweetie," she would say to me, her tone gentle like a summer breeze, "But you must believe with all your heart."

Those forgotten moments with my mother were coming back, such bittersweet memories, their warmth a stark of contrast to the emptiness I now faced. I could almost hear her voice whispering through the years, urging me to find happiness, find my joy, amidst my sorrow.

But my thoughts returned back to that dreadful night, a fateful night, when I received this gift of the mirror from Melissa, a night that had changed everything. It remained the most vivid memory, even now. As my mother's memories flooded my mind, while I held this fragile mirror in my hands, I remembered it all, finally, it all surfaced. I remembered being sick, a fragile wisp of a child, my body wracked with much pain, the oppressive darkness of the room that horrid night, the distant sound of my mother's voice mingling with the frantic whispers of the frightful doctor. I had thought I was slipping away, dying, trapped in a haze of fever and fear. And then, there was Melissa, appearing like a cloaked figure in the shadow of the night, like a mystery being, her dark hair, ravenously black, cascading like a waterfall around her. She knelt beside my bed next to me, her gaze penetrating yet soothing, as she held a finger to my lips, draped with a drop of her blood, "Just a few drops, my child. This will heal you."

Even though, I sensed the gravity of her actions, I wasn't fully afraid of her, as I greedily sucked the drops of blood from her finger. My mother had stirred, who slept next to me, her eyes fluttering open as she saw what was happening, "No! What are you doing to my daughter? Who are you?" My mother cried out, but it was too late.

Melissa's fangs pierced my mother's vein in her neck, and I watched in horror as the life was drained from her. Frozen still with such fright, I could not move. The blood, my lifeline, mingled with the horror of what I had just witnessed felt grotesque, a cruel twist of fate that bound me to Melissa in ways I could never understand. In that moment, I felt the world fracture, my heart breaking for my mother, even as my own body surged with vitality Melissa bestowed upon me. After it was over, after my mother lay lifeless on the bed next to me, I was enveloped in Melissa's firm embrace, "You're safe now, my dear," she whispered, her voice like a haunting lullaby, "You will not be alone. I will always be with you, now, and I will take care of you."

In that moment of despair, amidst the shadows of such loss, I found an anchor in her promise, a savior, a mentor. Melissa took me in, raised me as her own, and I clung to her as I would a lifeline. The brothel house became my new home, a place where I could begin to forget, to learn the nuances of my new life.

Yet even as the years passed, I never forgot the sacrifice that had forged our bond, the lives intertwined by love and loss, and the silver mirror, heavy in my hand, now reflected not just my image but the weight of my entire history. It was a reminder of the paths I had walked, the choices I was forced to make, and the indelible mark of those I had lost along the way. For some strange reason, another one of Melissa's stories surfaced in my mind...

'This is about a love that transcends life and death, set against the timeless beauty of Sicily. A woman named Aurelia, was a spirited being of Sicilian descent, encountering an enigmatic vampire named Vittorio. Despite the barriers between their worlds, their love grew. Aurelia becomes pregnant, igniting a mix of impossible hope and fear, but tragedy strikes during childbirth. Vittorio is left devastated as she and their unborn child slip away. Overwhelmed by eternal grief, he chooses to end his immortal existence in the same sun-drenched landscape where they had shared their love.

Within the small Sicilian village of Italy, legends of strange and enchanting figures roamed as commonly as the warm breeze. Aurelia, a young, beautiful, woman known for her curiosity and great beauty, had heard the stories since she was a child. The villagers spoke od specters who walked at night, cursed to wander until the end of time. She dismissed these as silly tales meant to keep children indoors after dusk, but one fateful evening, as the sun slipped below the horizon, she met Vittorio.

Vittorio was unlike anyone she'd ever seen. His face was hauntingly beautiful, with eyes that glimmered like moonlight on the Mediterranean. His voice was low and like velvet, and his presence exuded an aura of sorrow and wisdom. Drawn by an inexplicable force, Aurelia found herself entranced. She noticed his cold skin, the way he avoided the sun's touch, and the peculiar silence that fell whenever he approached. In the depths of her heart, she sensed he was one of those spectral beings from legend, yet her fear was mingled with something dangerously close to yearning. Each evening, Aurelia found herself wandering to the cliffside, where Vittorio often appeared to watch the stars. The two would speak of life, eternity, and many lost dreams. For Vittorio, who had walked through centuries, her vibrant view on life was a balm to his undying soul, and for Aurelia, his mystery and gentleness were like an addictive elixir. What began as a fleeting curiosity quickly grew into a passion that neither could resist.

Over time, Aurelia's affection for Vittorio blossomed into something so consuming that it defied reason. She could see past the chilling truths of his existence, his curse of eternity, and the cruel darkness he carried. The village murmured about the strange young man that she spent her evenings with, yet Aurelia paid them no mind. The entire island could turn against her, and she would still rather choose him. One evening, under the full moon's glow, Vittorio finally confessed his true nature. He spoke of his curse, his eternal hunger for blood, human blood, and the solitude that plagued him through the many ages. Aurelia listened, undeterred. She saw through his pain and only grew more determined to be closer to him. "If I have only a mortal's time to love you, then so be it," she declared with fierce loyalty.

Vittorio was astounded, terrified, and profoundly moved. Against all his better judgement, he yielded to the mortal love that Aurelia offered. For months, they lived in secret joy, their affections, their love a delicate flower, blossoming in the dark shadows. Each kiss, each intimate touch, felt more vibrant, knowing it could be their last, and then, one night, they discovered she was with child. Vittorio could sense the new blood, hear the faint heartbeat of another inside her.

The news was as miraculous as it was terrifying. Vittorio had never imagined that such a thing was even possible. His kind, his undead immortality, he believed, could not create life. Yet, here she was, Aurelia, his beloved, carrying a child within her, who was a part of him. The pregnancy brought its share of challenges. Aurelia's strength ebbed, her once-bright spirit seeming to slowly dim as her body struggled to bear the child of a vampire. Vittorio tried to mask his fear, staying by her side, as he struggled to contain his blood hunger, bringing her remedies, and searching desperately for any means to ensure her survival, and that of the unborn child. Deep within, he knew this child would demand more from Aurelia's mortal body than she could endure. The very thing that should have been a symbol of their love was now becoming a threat.

Despite Aurelia's failing health, she cherished the child growing inside her. She would touch her sensitive belly and smile, dreaming of a child who would carry both her heart and Vittorio's eternity. She whispered to him of a life together, one where they could be a real family, but Vittorio could only listen in silence, his heart splintering with the knowledge that she was slipping further from him each night. When the time finally came, Aurelia's frail body could not withstand the agony of the childbirth. She fought bravely, clutching Vittorio's hand, her breath coming in desperate gasps. Vittorio, who had seen death in countless forms, had never known such fear as he did now. The silence that fell when her breath ceased was the cruelest sound he had ever heard.

The small room was filled with a chilling quietness as Vittorio held the still, lifeless form of the child. His undead heart shattered with every second, the weight of his endless immortal life pressing down like a tombstone. Aurelia's peaceful face looked like she was merely asleep, yet he knew she was forever gone. The love he had cherished, the warmth that had soothed his immortal soul, had slipped away from him for all eternity. For several hours, Vittorio lingered by her side, haunted by memories of her laughter, the way she had called him back from his desolation. Now, those moments were gone, leaving him with nothing but an eternity of emptiness. He held her cold, lifeless hand to his lips, whispering a final goodbye, his voice broken by much sorrow. As he gently placed the small, fragile, lifeless child next to the mother, Vittorio shed a blood tear down his face.

In his despair, Vittorio's thoughts grew darker within him, he knew he could not endure the endless stretch of time without her. Aurelia had been his only tether to the world, the only light in his dark existence. Now that light was gone, and with it, the desire to continue, to even exist. At dawn, as the sun began to rise over the rolling hills of Sicily, Vittorio walked to the cliffside where they had first met. The sky turned from black to a delicate shade of purple, then a bright orange, as the sun prepared to crest the horizon. He could feel its warmth drawing closer, a reminder of the mortal life he had left behind centuries ago, a life that he could no longer bear to endure without Aurelia. As Vittorio stood in the first light of dawn, he took a final breath. He welcomed the sun's fatal touch, feeling his skin begin to burn, the curse of his existence melting away in a fiery embrace. It was both agony and a release, a final sacrifice to join the woman he had loved beyond reason. His last thoughts were of Aurelia, of the beautiful child they would never raise together, and of the love he would always carry with him into oblivion. With the morning light completely consuming him, Vittorio found a peace at last, as his spirit merged with the warmth of the sun that rose over Sicily, an eternal love story, sealed by the sun's last embrace. Just a tragic romance, where the boundless love between a vampire and a mortal woman is ultimately torn apart by the laws of nature and the limitations of morality. Set in the enchanting landscapes of Sicily, the love story resonates with both timeless beauty and profound sorrow, illustrating that not even the undead can escape the pain of love and loss.'

I regretfully remembered so much more, as I reflected back, when Melissa confessed her truth, her long held secrets, to me that dreadful night...

Chapter 8

I gazed through the window, as all the forgotten memories of my mother still lingered fresh in my mind, watching the full moon shine brightly above. The light peering, cascading over the deserted streets below, where men and women had bustled about their usual routines just hours earlier. Inside the brothel house, I stood with Melissa across the room, a room dimly lit by a single candlestick burning in sequence with the almost void breeze. Its dim glow casting a golden glow over the plush furniture of the room. An elegant silence hung between Melissa and me, as she relaxed in the armchair that seemed to have been there as long as the brothel house itself. Melissa gracefully reclined with a certain grace, a calmness, with her legs crossed, one arm lazily draped over the side of the chair as she nursed a glass of red wine. She was the epitome of control, poised and unfazed by the silence of the world outside, her emerald eyes reflecting a depth of secrets still hidden for what seemed like centuries. As I stood there, my mind boiled with anger as the memories flooded my brain, my long-forgotten memories of my mother, my sickness, but I did not want the confrontation of what Melissa might really be, some kind of a monster who murdered my mother. 'Could my memories be the truth, or was my mind simply playing a cruel trick on me?'

Melissa was completely unaware of the thoughts raging through my head, she did not realize the 'memories' that this little gift of the legendary mirror had given me. I eased to the armchair next to Melissa, as I shifted in my seat, pushing aside a lock of my black hair behind my ear, my gaze turning to Melissa, as I still held tightly to the silver mirror. Thoughts of how long I have lived here in this brothel house, within these old walls, yet there was a part of Melissa that remained a dark mystery. The bond we shared was undeniable, complicated, rich with unspoken understanding, but still, I felt there was something about Melissa that eluded her. Trying my best to contain my frustrations, I took a deep breath, and said, "Melissa," I began as soft as I could, my voice breaking the comfortable silence in the room, "Have you ever believed in love, at all?"

Melissa raised a curious eyebrow, the faintest smile playing at the corners of her lips. She swirled the wine in her glass, eyes fixed on the rich, red fluid before her gaze flicked up to meet my firm stare, "Love?" she repeated, her voice as smooth as the silk robe that draped over her pale shoulders, "What makes you ask such a thing, my dear?"

I smiled faintly, a small hint of frustration still lingering, pulling my legs beneath me as I settled more comfortably into my armchair, "I don't know, really. It's been on my mind for a while, lately." My eyes looking toward the window, but I did not focus on what lay beyond, "I watch the girls, in the parlor of the brothel, you know? The ones that come and go from here. Some of them talk about love as if it's the most important thing in the world, while the others, like it's a fairytale. I guess I'm just curious about you think, I mean, since you were against my relationship, my love for Patrick."

Melissa's smile widened slightly, as she rolled her eyes, though they held a shadow of something darker, something more knowing. She leaned forward slightly, her eyes piercing, though still soft in the dim light, "Love, my sweet Maria Grace, is perhaps the most misunderstood force in existence."

I felt a shiver run down my spine, though I wasn't exactly sure why, "Misunderstood?"

Melissa nodded, "Oh yes. You see, people believe that love is this pure, untainted thing, a feeling that uplifts and transforms, but love is far more complicated than that, Maria Grace. It's powerful, yes, but it's also selfish, dangerous. It can destroy as easily as it can heal, and about all the other girls here in the brothel, I care not about their love affairs. I only care for you and your well-being."

I tilted my head, considering Melissa's words, "But you believe in it, in love?"

Melissa took as low sip of her red wine before setting the glass down on the small table beside her armchair. She ran a finger along the rim of the glass thoughtfully, "I believe in many things, my dear, love is one of them, but it's not the way people like to think of it. They imagine it as eternal, unconditional. In my experience, love is much like life, fleeting, something that can turn brutal, though often beautiful, yet always temporary."

My heart ached at that, though I wasn't entirely sure why. There was something almost tragic in the way Melissa spoke about love, as if it were a thing she hadn't known intimately but lost long ago.

"You've been in love before, haven't you, Melissa." I said softly, more a statement than a question.

Melissa's eyes grew distant, her lips pressing together in a tight line. For a moment, I thought she wouldn't answer me, but then she let out a soft sigh, her eyes flickering with something ancient, something that carried the weight of what seemed like centuries, "Yes," she said simply, "Many times, in fact, but love, for someone like me, is never quite what it seems. It always comes with a price."

I furrowed my brow, curiosity bubbling up inside me, "What do you mean, 'someone like you'?"

Melissa's gaze sharpened suddenly, but the intensity faded as quick as it had appeared, replaced with her usual calm, enigmatic demeanor. She smiled, a small, almost sad smile, and reached out, brushing a strand of my hair behind my ear, the gesture so gentle that it made my heart flutter, "Someday. you will understand, Maria Grace," Melissa said quietly, her voice almost a faint whisper, "But for now, let's just say that love and I... we are old acquaintances."

My chest tightened with a deep longing that I could not quite explain. I had known Melissa for as long as I could remember, and I realized there was still so many things I did not know or understand. Melissa had always been there, always taken care of me, since the day I had been brought into this brothel house, a sickly child, healed by her blood, with no family to call my own, and no future. Melissa had gave me a future, she had saved me, healed me, given me a life that I wouldn't have had otherwise. And yet, there was always that sense of distance, as though Melissa existed in a world apart from the one, I inhabited, and the questions still remained in my head about the recent flood of memories of that night when my mother died, and Melissa healed me with her blood. 'Why did her blood heal me? Was there any truth to these memories in my mind?'

"You took me in when I had nowhere else to go," I said, my voice nervous, "You've always been there for me. I guess I wonder sometimes... why?"

Melissa's emerald eyes softened, and for the briefest moment, there was something much like vulnerability in her gaze, something I had never seen before, "I saw something in you, Maria Grace," Melissa replied, her voice low, "Something... special."

I blinked, surprised by the intensity in Melissa's response, her mere tone, "Special?"

Melissa nodded, her hand falling to her lap as she leaned back in her armchair, "You were so young, so fragile, but there was a strength in you, in your eyes, a resilience. I knew that, given the chance at life, you could grow into someone remarkable, and I was not wrong."

I felt my cheeks begin to flush at the compliment, but there was still a lingering question, one I couldn't shake, "But why me? I wasn't the only child out there, there were other children, others who needed help, or others who could be stronger than I was. Why did you have to choose me?"

Melissa's eyes darkened, her gaze flicking away for a moment as if she were searching for the right words to say. When she spoke again, her voice was almost hesitant, faint, "Perhaps... because I saw a bit of myself in you."

My heart skipped a beat, my mind racing with the implications of those words. I had always felt an estranged connection to Melissa, something deeper than just gratitude for being taken in, but hearing Melissa admit that there was a personal reason behind it, a reflection of herself, stirred something in my soul. After feeling betrayed and hurt by Patrick, his disappearance, and the mere feelings of abandonment by him, I realized that Melissa was all I had to cling to. Melissa stood from her armchair, abruptly, walking over to the window where I had stood earlier, still holding her glass of red wine. She just stood there, looking out the window, staring out at the darkened sky, her posture tense, as though she were holding back some great truths.

I've lived a long time, my dear," Melissa said finally, her voice serene, but filled with deep emotion, "Longer than you can imagine, and in that time, I've seen things, felt things, and lost things. I've gained much wisdom about love, about people, and about life, even the lack thereof."

I stood up too, slowly moving toward Melissa at the window, hesitating for a moment before reaching out and gently placing my hand on her arm, "You don't have to tell me everything you've been through," I said in a whisper, "But I am here, and I am listening. If you choose to tell me of your past affections, I'm all ears, and I will try to understand."

Melissa's shoulders relaxed slightly, and she turned her head to look at me. There was something raw in her stare, something vulnerable and ancient, and for the first time, I saw a glimpse of the heaviness Melissa carried within her, the weight of what seems like lifetimes lived and tragically lost.

" I took you in because I could not bear to lose another," Melissa whispered. "Not after..." Her voice fading off, but the silence that followed was extremely heavy with much unspoken pain.

My heart ached more for her, for this saddened woman with her secrets, who had been my protector, my guardian, for as long as I could remember. She had always been so strong, untouchable, in my eyes, but now, I realized that there was so much more beneath the surface, so much more pain, so much untold history hid behind her emerald eyes.

"Melissa," I said, "You don't have to carry it all alone, anymore."

Melissa smiled faintly, though her smile never reached her eyes, "I've carried it for so long, now, Maria Grace. I do not know any other way."

I took a deep breath, gathering my courage, "You can tell me, Melissa. Whatever it is, I won't judge you for it."

For a moment, it seemed like Melissa might actually open up to me, that she might finally reveal her secrets that had been weighing her down for what seemed like centuries, but then, as quickly as the vulnerability had appeared, it vanished, replaced by the familiar mask of control and elegance that Melissa always wore.

"Perhaps another time. It's getting late, and you should get some rest, Maria Grace." Melissa said with a gentle smile, as she took the last sip of her red wine.

I wanted to protest, to convince Melissa that she didn't need to keep her distance from me, that she needed to release her secrets, her pain, but I knew that pushing too hard would only make her retreat further. So, instead, I nodded, though my heart felt heavy with the weight of everything unsaid, "Goodnight, Melissa," I said quietly.

"Goodnight, Maria Grace."

As I left the room, the feeling of something unresolved lingered in the air. I knew that there was so much more to Melissa's story, so much more to our story, but for now, it would remain hidden in the shadows, just out of reach.

I lay in bed that night, restless, my thoughts swirling with everything Melissa had said, and all the memories circling in my mind about my mother, along with Melissa's take on love, life, and whatever secrets she held hidden, locked away. It was strange, living in this place like this, surrounded by the noise and the chaos of the brothel and the girls within in it, yet finding myself consumed by deeper, quieter thoughts. The girls who lived here with us were loud often times, brash at other times, but they carried their own burdens, keeping to their selves. Some of them spoke of love as if it were a fleeting fantasy, while others clung to it desperately, hoping it would save them from the life they led. But I had always been different than the 'girls' of the brothel house, perhaps it was because I had grown up under Melissa's protective wing, sheltered in a way the other girls hadn't been. I had known love, my Patrick had showed it to me, but now, he was gone away, yet I still cannot comprehend why he would leave behind the way he did. My mind remembered the night Melissa had found me, it was faint memory of late, yet in it was so vivid now, like a reoccurring dream, a blur of pain and fear. My childish body weak and feverish, lying in the cold bed, I had been dying, though I hadn't understood that at the time. Then Melissa had appeared, like an angel of mercy, a dark angel of cruel mercy, though now, I realized that perhaps, she was something else entirely, something murderous. That night, Melissa had lifted me in her arms, cradling me like a child that I was, whispering something soft and soothing that I couldn't quite remember. There had been a sharp pain, just for a moment, while in Melissa's arms, and then a warmth that spread through my body, healing me, saving me. I passed out, but when I awoke the next evening, I was in the brothel house, and Melissa was there next me, watching over me. For years, I had believed it was simply a miracle, something miraculous that I couldn't explain, but was endlessly grateful for, but now, as I lay in my bed, thinking back on that night, I couldn't shake the feeling that there was more to it than I had ever known. I pondered on the way Melissa spoke about life and about love, about the heaviness she carried within her. I thought of the strange intensity in Melissa's eyes when she talked about loss, about seeing herself in me.

 The thoughts of blood swirled in my head, as I pondered on the memory that revealed itself to me this night, when I looked in the vintage mirror that Melissa had given me, I traced my delicate fingertips across the edges, thoughts of my mother's death seemed clearer. The blood had only been a drop, a small, crimson bead on Melissa's fingertip. I hadn't questioned it at the time, had barely noticed in my feverish state, since I was so young and hardly able to hold a deep breath, but now, as the memory replayed in my mind, it felt like the key to something much larger, something I had been too small to understand.

'What had Melissa done to me that horrid night? To my mother?' I turned and tossed in bed for what seemed like hours, as all this rolled around in my thoughts, pulling the covers up to my chin, my mind raced with unanswered questions. I knew Melissa had definitely saved my life, that much was certain, but at what cost? 'Was my mother's life the price that needed to be paid? And why had she chosen me?' Sure, she said she saw herself in me, but it just did not add up in my head, as to why she would save me. 'What of my Patrick, did he just leave me, really leave me behind, or was it far worse a fate?' These questions circled in my head all night; it seemed. All this weighed heavy on my heart as I finally drifted off to sleep with tears in my eyes, the darkness of the room, the silence, wrapping around me like a shroud. In the quiet of the night, with only soft sounds of the brothel house settling around me, I dreamed of blood and dark shadows, of love and loss, and of a secret that lay just beneath the surface, waiting to be uncovered.

The next evening, I gained a sense of determination. I had always put my trust in Melissa, had always believed in her kindness toward me, her mere strength of a woman, but now, I began to realize that there was more to our estranged relationship than I had ever known, and I couldn't be silent, or ignore it, any longer. The little silver mirror she had given me, made it clear, Melissa was hiding the truth from me.

I found Melissa in the kitchenette, sipping her usual evening tea of rosemary herbs, her expression calm and composed as always, but I could see the faint tension in her pale shoulders, the way her fingers drummed lightly against the small table she was sitting next to, as if she were lost in deep thought.

"Melissa," I said quietly, approaching the table, "we need to talk."

Melissa looked up, her expression unreadable, "About what, my dear?"

"About me, about us," I replied, my voice nervous, yet steady. "About the night you saved me."

Melissa's eyes flickered with a twinkle of shock, yet a knowingness, and for a moment, there was a silence between us, heavy and full of unspoken truths.

"What is it that you want to know, Maria Grace?" Melissa asked finally, her voice low, as she sipped more of her tea.

I took a deep breath, gathering my courage, "I want to know the truth, Melissa."

She placed her teacup down on the fragile table, her emerald eyes locking onto mine with an intensity that made my heart race. The air in the room seemed to grow heavier, and for the first time, I felt a hint of fear. But Melissa simply nodded, a faint, almost sad smile playing at her lips, "Very well, Maria Grace. You deserve to know the truth, but before I speak of it, just know, I was a lonely being for many, many centuries, and I saw a comfort in you."

As Melissa began to speak, I felt my world shift, the foundation of everything I had once believed beginning to crumble to dust. We made our way to the balcony of the brothel house, as Melissa led the way with my hand in hers. She led the conversation with a tale, a romantic tragedy, her usual way of telling me stories, except this tale seemed to be told a little strangely...

'Whispers of the Crescent Moon... within the vibrant yet eerie streets of the French Quarter in New Orleans. Its lively streets, shadowy alleys, and hauntingly beautiful architecture, provides the perfect atmosphere for this tale of forbidden love. Susan, a young witch with a fierce spirit and a deep connection to the natural world. She is known for her herbal remedies and enchantments but struggles with the stigma of her craft in a community that fears magic. Then there is Anthony, a brooding vampire, centuries old, who has wandered through the dark alleys of New Orleans, searching for redemption from his past. He is drawn to the city's mystique and its rich, tragic history.

As the sun sets over the French Quarter, casting long shadows over the cobblestone streets, Susan brews her potions in her modest little shop, surrounded by jars of herbs and mystical artifacts. One evening, she encounters Anthony, who is drawn to her shop by the scent of her magic. Their connection is immediate, a spark igniting between the witch and the vampire, two lost souls caught in a web of cruel fate. Despite the danger of their relationship, vampires and witches are said to be sworn enemies, they find themselves irresistibly drawn to one another. They meet in secret, sharing stolen moments in the moonlit courtyards of the Quarter, exchanging dreams and fears. Susan teaches Anthony about the beauty of an ancient prophecy: a witch and a vampire united in love would lead to chaos, risking the balance between their two worlds. Conflicted yet determined, Susan decides to confront the prophecy. In a moment of passion, they promise to defy fate, believing their mere love can conquer all, but as the Crescent Moon rises, an unforeseen betrayal occurs. Susan's best friend, consumed by jealousy and fear, reveals their secret to the community. In a furious confrontation, the elders of the witch coven and the vampires within the Quarter unite to punish the two lovers. In a tragic twist of fate, Anthony is cursed to roam the earth forever, alone, a shadow of his former self, while Susan is bound by her coven, her powers, her magic, stripped away. Their final meeting is a heart-wrenching farewell under the stars, where they confess their undying love. They share a bittersweet kiss, knowing they can never be together again, and promise to find each other in another life. As the moon wanes, Susan watches Anthony fade into the night, his figure disappearing into the shadows of the French Quarter. Heartbroken, she returns to her empty shop, surrounded by the remnants of their love. The memory of their passionate encounters lingers, and she vows to honor their love by keeping their story alive through her dead magic. In the end, their love story becomes a whispered legend in the French Quarter, a tale of a witch and a vampire whose forbidden love echoed through time, reminding all who heard it, of the delicate balance between love and fate, and the tragedy that comes from defying it. This is how it all happened...

In the shadows of the Quarter, the sun dipped below the horizon, casting a warm orange glow over the cobblestone streets of the French Quarter. Music drifted through the air, mingling with the sweet scent of lavender and jasmine, and the rich aroma of Cajun cuisine. In a little modest shop tucked between vibrant old buildings, Susan mixed her herbal brews, her fingers dancing deftly among the jars lining the shelves. A flicker of movement caught her eye. A tall figure leaned against the doorframe; a silhouette shrouded in shadow. It was Anthony, his piercing gaze reflecting the last light of the day. Susan felt her heart race; she had seen him wandering the Quarter, an enigma wrapped in darkness, yet this was the first time their paths had truly crossed. "Can I help you?" she asked, her voice steady despite the fluttering in her chest.

Anthony stepped into the dim light, revealing high cheekbones and a smirk that hinted at mischief, "I was drawn here by something... magical."

Their conversations unfolded over the following weeks like the petals of a blooming flower. In the secret corners of the Quarter, they shared laughter and dreams, a bond growing stronger with each stolen moment. Susan introduced Anthony to the enchantment of her magical world, showing him the beauty of herbs and the art of potion-making. One evening, as they wandered through a quiet courtyard, Susan turned to him, her heart pounding, "Why do you linger here, Anthony?" What are you searching for?"

Anthony paused, his gaze intense, "Redemption, perhaps. A reason to feel alive again, instead of this evil, undead creature of the night, that I am now."

Their fingers brushed, sending sparks of energy between them. The world around them faded, and in that moment, nothing else mattered. As their love deepened, Susan unearthed a prophecy hidden in her coven's ancient texts. She had hoped to ignore it, to believe in their love alone, but the words haunted her: 'A witch and a vampire united shall bring chaos, their love a curse upon the world. Only bringing unbalance and danger.'

Fear gripped Susan's heart, "Anthony, what if we are destined for only darkness?"

He cupped her face, his touch gentle yet firm, "Then we will fight it together. Our love can conquer any fate, can it not? Besides, I have always lived within my own darkness for many centuries."

But doubt lingered with Susan, creeping into their shared moments like a shadow. One fateful night, as they met beneath the glow of the Crescent Moon, the atmosphere shifted. The air crackled with tension; something was amiss. Susan's heart sank as her best friend,

Elara, appeared, eyes wide with fear and anger, yet a hint of jealousy. Elara was her friend from the coven that she was a part of. "I can't believe you!" Elara shouted. "You're risking everything being with him, a vampire!"

Before Susan could respond, Elara had already run off, leaving a trail of whispers behind her. Panic surged through Susan as the hard reality of their love's danger settled in. The supernatural laws would never accept them, this love affair. Days passed, the streets of the French Quarter feeling heavier with each moment. Whispers of a witch's betrayal grew louder, and soon, the elders of Susan's coven summoned both her and Anthony, along with other ancient witches and vampires within the Quarter. Under the flickering gaslights of the coven's secret chambers, Susan stood beside Anthony, her heart racing, nervous. The tension was palpable as the leaders of the coven glared at the two lovers, a storm of fury brewing in the air. "Your love, your union, defies the natural order of life!" The head elder of the coven declared, voice echoing in the stillness, as all the other witches nodded in agreement, along with the ancient vampires. "You must end this union at once, you must be punished for your betrayal against the law of nature and your coven."

In an instant, chaos erupted. Anthony stepped forward, eyes blazing with much determination, "We will not be torn apart by your threats. We will not be broken by such fear."

But their defiance only fueled the elder's wrath. Susan watched in horror as spells flew, and in a moment of darkness, Anthony was struck by a powerful curse, the light in his eyes dimming. As the other ancient vampires made their leave, along with all the witch elders of the coven, Susan, heartbroken, rushed to Anthony's side as the coven's magic still wrapped around him like a shroud. "No! Please!" she cried, warm tears streaming down her cheeks.

Anthony looked at her, pain etched across his undead features, "Susan... I will always love you. I will always search for a way to be with you."

In their final moments together, they exchanged promises and confessions, sealing their love with a desperate kiss under the Crescent Moon. As their lips parted, Anthony began to fade, shadows consuming him. "I will find you again," he whispered, his voice barely audible as he vanished into the night, his spirit cursed to wander the Quarter alone.

Susan sadly returned to her little shop, surrounded by silence and faint memories. The air was heavy with much sorrow, but she knew she had to honor their love, to remember Anthony and his embrace. She poured her heart into her dead magic, creating over and over again, her potions and charms that whispered their story to anyone willing to listen. Finally, after many attempts, her magic returned to her, as if it never left. In the quiet of her heart, Susan vowed to keep their love alive, telling the tale of a witch and a vampire whose bond defied fate. The streets of the French Quarter echoed with their legacy, a reminder that love, no matter how tragic, could transcend time and darkness. And as the Crescent Moon rose high in the night sky, Susan closed her eyes, feeling the warmth of Anthony's presence surround her, a lingering promise of hope in a world that once sought to tear them apart. She would find a way to be with him again, her vampire, her only love.'

The memory of this conversation still floods my mind, though, after her sad, tragic story, Melissa did not confess to everything... Yet, it was the conversation that followed month's after, one tense evening that changed everything...

Chapter 9

Standing on that balcony, I patiently waited, as Melissa poured the truth from her lips, of my survival, my mother's death, and how she felt awful afterwards. I felt angered, yet I already accepted this truth when I learned of it through the vintage, silver mirror she had given me. Melissa confessed with much sorrowfulness, yet she never shed one tear. She hugged me tightly and said her apologies, as she left me there standing on the balcony alone. Overwhelmed, I still had questions that I needed answered, about Patrick, and why did she refer to 'centuries' in her response to me. 'Was Melissa something of evil, or was she 'immortal'? Could such things really exist?' These thoughts played in my mind for several nights thereafter, with Melissa dodging me. She would always be too busy to speak of such things with me...

It took months before Melissa's full truth unfurled, a truth entwined with what she had already confessed to me about my mother's death, a truth she entwined with the very essence of who she was. For so long, I lived in blissful ignorance, wrapped in the cocoon of our unnatural bond together, I was like her daughter, her companion in the shadowy corridors of the brothel house. Without fully understanding the implications of my being, I was foolish, it seemed, to believe Melissa could truly care for me, the way I did for her all these blinded years.

I reflect back on Melissa's words she had once spoke to me, yet I did not ever understand them until now... "'Watching people, different shapes and sizes. Some happy, some sad," Melissa said vaguely, as she was lost in deep thought, one late night as we lingered in the parlor alone, "Some in pain, some in complete misery, it all challenges me not to end their suffering as I gaze upon such pathetic beings. You know, Maria Grace, vampires do exist, they have morals, and value human existence. They only kill to survive as the evil creature they are cursed to be. Vampires still feel sadness, loneliness, and such-like emotions. Some of these creatures take years to learn such things...'"

Melissa's words still ring in my head, although, I could not understand them back then, I fully comprehend them now. All those years ago, I merely thought that Melissa was intrigued with the fantasy of vampires, yet now, I know she was one all along, as I am now.

Finally, Melissa confessed the whole truth about my Patrick...

It was on a stormy night, the rain pounding against the window of the brothel house, that the dam of secrets finally broke. I had grown restless with her always avoiding me of late, a simmering unease brewing within me as I listened to the fierce, beating rain, and in the flickering candlelight of the parlor, I confronted her, "Melissa, what really happened to Patrick? I mean, I cannot believe he just disappeared, leaving me behind."

The question hung heavy in the air, a portent of the unraveling that was about to happen, yet I had to know the truth, I just couldn't hold these unanswered questions inside any longer. Melissa's eyes seemed to darken, I could see the weight of her untold history in those emerald depths of her eyes, "I never meant for you to find out in this way, Maria Grace," she said, her voice a haunting melody, "but you do deserve to know the whole truth, the truth about your love, Patrick."

With each word, she peeled back the layers of her past, revealing the darkest corners of our intertwined lives. She spoke of the night Patrick had supposedly disappeared, of her jealously, her fear of detachment from me, "I could not stand to see you so happy. I knew he would pull you away from me, it was the only way to keep you by my side."

The admission felt like ice flooding my veins, a shattering truth that sent my heart racing. Part of me was hoping Melissa hadn't taken his life, yet I knew within myself it was so. I needed no explanation as to how she did it, all I needed to understand was my Patrick was murdered by the hand of my protector, Melissa.

"And my mother?" I could barely utter the words, yet they spilled from my lips like poison. "Did you have to take her life, was it really necessary?"

"I had to save you, Maria Grace," Melissa faintly whispered, a desperate edge in her tone, "Your mother... you were dying, and I offered you a chance at life, but it did come with a price. I had no choice, your mother would've never allowed me to keep you, I had to have you for my own."

As the weight of her confession settled over me, I ran my fingertips over the vintage mirror in my dress pocket, nervously, the walls closed in around me, and I felt as if I could not breathe, the air grew thick with much betrayal. The love I had once felt for Melissa twisted into something much darker, more complex, hatred. I was no longer like a daughter to her, I was just a pawn in her whirlwind of a life's game, just an echo of the life she must've taken from others before me. In that moment of painful clarity, something inside me shifted. Rage coursed through my veins like wildfire, igniting a primal instinct that had long been dormant, "You took everything from me! It would've been better for you to let me die that horrid night, Melissa!" I cried, my voice rising above the storm. "You killed my mother! You destroyed my love, Patrick, and now you want me to understand it was all done out of love for me! You needed me for yourself!"

The confrontation spiraled into chaos, the candlelight flickered wildly as the lightening outside grew more intense, as emotions surged between us, and then, in a blur of desperation and anger, I found myself reaching for the rusty dagger that lay on the fragile vanity table, a relic from the past, stained with Melissa's memories, and unknown blood. It was a fateful moment, the culmination of years of hidden pain and untold truths. As I plunged the rusty dagger into her chest, straight through her heart, time seemed to stretch into eternity. Melissa's eyes widened in shock, yet there was a glimmer of understanding in them, a recognition that this was the end of our twisted journey together.

"Maria Grace," she gasped, as blood bubbled from her lips, the strength draining from her body.

In one last attempt, Melissa buried her fangs, something I had never knew she had, into my neck, just barely missing my main artery. Pushing her weakened body away from me, the blood stained my hands, her blood mingled with my own, but the blood that was spilled between us now, wasn't just mere blood; it was the weight of our shared history, the sacrifices made, and the irrevocable choices that had led us to this horrible moment. Melissa's emerald eyes dulled, faded, the life ebbing away as her body dropped from my arms. I knelt beside her, my heart ponding in my chest with grief and fury.

In her last moments, as her body slumped over on the wooded floor, I saw a glimpse of the beauty I had once knew, a beauty that had long ago captivated me. Melissa lay there, lifeless, stiff, and yet serene, like a fallen star caught in the night, her glassy gaze forever searching for something lost. The vintage, silver mirror she had gifted me with lay unshattered beside us, obviously falling from my dress pocket in the chaos, a fragment reflecting the room's dark corners, a reminder of the life I had chosen, the memory of a gift that was given in love, the sacrifices made all in the name of love. I, now, had Melissa's blood, her life, stained on my own hands. As I wiped my lips with my fingers, overwhelmed at the scene that had just taken place, this little, small gesture changed my life forever. Her blood, mingled with my mortal blood, was now inside of me, as I realized what I had just done. As the realization of what Melissa truly was, an immortal killer, sank into my head, I felt the change, the transformation, beginning within my body. "Goodbye Melissa, my protector, my estranged lover." I whispered faintly, as her body faded into ashes, floating up into the air of the room.

With Melissa's death, a profound silence enveloped the room, a silence that echoed through the halls of the brothel house, which is now, a hotel, a silence that would linger for decades. I was left alone with only my memories, haunted by choices that had shaped my mere existence, and the realization that I was now an eternal being in a world where love and loss were intertwined. Melissa had been a vampire, an immortal creature, and I never knew her secret until that fateful night. All her stories, her tales, her poems, had been a reflection of her saddened past.

One such story surfaces in my mind that Melissa once told me...

'Shadows of Loneliness'... 'In the early 1500's, Paris was a city of contrasts, a vibrant tapestry of life and art woven through narrow, winding streets, yet beneath the lively exterior lay a deep current of sorrow. The rain fell incessantly, drumming against the cobblestones outside Lucille's modest lodging, a small room overlooking the Seine. The flickering candlelight cast long shadows, dancing across the floral walls adorned with fading tapestries, remnants of a once-vibrant life now marred by such loneliness. Lucille sat in her dimly lit room, her heart saddened, heavy with the weight of solitude. She wrapped herself in a tattered shawl, the fabric frayed and threadbare, a testament to her dwindling means. In one hand, she held a delicate glass filled with cheap red wine, its deep crimson hue mirroring the ache within her. Each sip offered a fleeting escape from the bitter reality of her sad life, a brief respite from the gnawing emptiness that had become her most constant companion. The grand city of love bustled outside her fragile window, with the sounds of faint laughter and merriment wafting through the air. Artists displayed their majestic works in the nearby square, musicians strummed lively tunes around every corner, and couples danced under the glow of lanterns. But for Lucille, the joy of the world felt as distant as the stars above, hidden behind the clouds of her despair.

As the evening deepened, the door to her room creaked open, revealing the figure of a man cloaked in a dark mantle. His name was Curtis, a musician with an enchanting voice and a heart full of passion. They had met in a nearby tavern, both seeking solace from their own sad troubles. He captivated Lucille with his music, the melodies flowing from his lute like water from a spring, refreshing her parched spirit. Curtis had seen her loneliness, had watched as she sipped her red wine, her eyes reflecting a deep sadness that echoed his own. He had approached her, a warm smile lighting up his face, and offered her a song, a melody that seemed to weave a thread of connection between them. "You need not be alone, my lady, my fair Lucille," he had said softly, his voice like pure velvet, but as the days turned into weeks, Lucille found herself retreating further into her saddened solitude. The bottle of wine had become her only confidant, the alcohol wrapping around her heart like a vice, stifling the flickers of hope that Curtis tried to ignite. She pushed him away, believing she was unworthy of the warmth he offered her, convinced that his light would only illuminate her inner sadness, her inner darkness.

"Lucille, please," Curtis implored one evening, his eyes searching hers with desperation that made her heart ache. "You do not have to bear your burdens alone. Allow me to be your companion in this storm that you hide within yourself."

She shook her head, warm tears spilling down her cheeks, "I am a wretched woman, a wretched creature, Curtis. I fear I will bring only sorrow to you."

Yet, Curtis remained steadfast. He visited her often, bringing gifts of various colored wildflowers from the countryside and sharing stories of his travels through much of France. He sang her enchanting songs that spoke of true love and beauty, his words wrapping around her like a comforting embrace, but Lucille, entrenched in her despair, could not see the love in his eyes, nor the beauty that he saw in her. One fateful night, after a day spent drowning in her sorrow, after much red wine was consumed, Lucille awoke from a restless sleep to find the streets alive with the sounds of celebration. A festival was underway, a tribute to the annual harvest, where townsfolk gathered to dance and revel beneath the moonlight, the full harvest moon. As she gazed out her window, the colors and the laughter spilled into her room, taunting her with what she could no longer have. With a sudden impulse, she slipped on a worn, faded dress and stepped into the night, the light, sprinkling rain mingling with the festivities. The festive music beckoned her, a siren's call that stirred a longing with her. As she wandered through the throng of people, she spotted Curtis on a small stage, his fingers dancing over the strings of his lute, his voice rising above the distant chatter of the crowd. He sang of love lost and found, of dreams and bitter despair, and Lucille felt her heart swell with a mixture of yearning and regret. She could see the joy in his masculine face, the way the crowd was drawn to him like moths to a flame. Yet, as he sang, his gaze drifted past the crowd, seeking her in the shadows. When their eyes met, a flicker of hope ignited within her, but just as quickly, she felt the weight of her own inadequacy pull her back into her inner darkness. With trembling hands, she turned away, slipping back into the night, the laughter of the crowd fading behind her. She stumbled through the rain-soaked streets, the cold water soaking the hem of her faded dress, but she felt nothing, not even the chill of the evening air. Her heart felt heavy, saddened, as if it were encased in iron shackles.

The next morning dawned with a bleak gray sky, and Lucille awoke to an emptiness that seemed to stretch beyond the walls of her frail room. The echoes of the previous night haunted her, the realization of her choices crashing down upon her. She reached for the bottle of red wine, the familiar burn, the familiar bitterness of the taste, in her throat offering the only comfort she knew, but the bottle felt heavier in her fragile, weakened hands, a burden she could no longer bear. Days turned into weeks, and the vibrant city continued to swirl around her, oblivious to her inner suffering. Curtis had tried to reach her, sending notes that went unanswered, flowers that withered in the corner of her deserted room, as she would allow him to see her. Each flower, a reminder of his presence, feeling like a dagger in her chest, a cruel reminder of the warmth she had pushed away.

One rain-soaked evening, as Lucille stared out at the Seine, she saw him again, Curtis, standing by the water's edge. His dark hair was damp, his eyes shadowed by sorrow. He played a mournful tune on his dampened lute, the notes drifting through the air like whispers of lost dreams. Lucille's heart ached at the sight of him. She wanted to call out to him, to explain the darkness that had consumed her, but fear held her captive. Instead, she only watched as he finished his song, a look of resignation settling on his masculine features before he turned away, the light fading behind him, leaving her once again in the shadows of her sorrow, never allowing her to ever see Curtis again. In that saddened moment, Lucille understood the true cost of her bitter loneliness, the loss of love, the shattering of hope. As she sank back into the depths of her utter despair, she realized that some choices could never be undone, and the inner darkness, her sadness, was now her only companion. Legend would say that Lucille consumed too much of her red wine, that she is now a spirit that still dwells in the fragile window of that room, overlooking the city of Paris.'

This tale of Lucille lingers in my mind as I remember the sad eyes of Melissa, yet they carried a sense of relief that fateful night that I took away her existence. I moved on in this eternal dance of survival. Yet, amidst this eternal dance of survival, within the winding streets of New Orleans, a city's rich tapestry of tragic history unfurls below me like the intricate patterns of a lace shawl. The scent of magnolia and jasmine hang heavy in the night air, mingling with the distant sound of jazz music that seeps through the cobblestone alleys. I can almost hear the whispers of the past echoing in the warm breeze of the night, a cacophony of lives once lived, loves lost, and secrets still buried deep within the shadows of the French Quarter. From its inception in the

1500's, New Orleans had always been a city steeped in contradiction, founded by the French, it became a melting pot of many cultures, Spanish, African, Creole, each contributing to the vibrant, chaotic beauty that defines it today. The streets tell the hidden stories of resilience, where those who sought refuge from oppression carved out their identities amidst the bustling markets and vibrant festivities, creating traditions to honor and remember their ancestors. The French Quarter, in particular, became a safe haven for artists, dreamers, and those who danced on the fringes of society, and I was here, watching, adapting, through it all. Through the decades, I watched, witnessed, as the ever-shifting landscape of the Quarter, this majestic city, began to change. The brothel house, my only known home, had flourished during a time long ago, when secrecy was essential, yet as, I alone, watched the 1900's approach, the mere atmosphere changed completely. The whispers of reform and morality swept through the streets like a storm, threatening to dismantle the very foundation on which my life was built. I had no choice but to adapt to these changes, trying to always stay a step ahead, while I remained in the shadows, looming, reminding myself of the fragility of my existence.

Now, as I look out at the vibrant, darkened streets of the French Quarter of New Orleans, I understand that the city itself is just a tapestry of tragedies and triumphs, woven together through the centuries, and like the city, I too am a creature of the shadows, shaped by the history that surrounds me, forever reflecting on the lives I touched over time, the lives I've taken, and the love I once knew and lost. The haunting echoes of the past that still whisper through the corridors of my immortal soul, I can't help but feel that Melissa had given me this vintage, silver mirror, I still hold in my hands, as a mere confession; for she knew it would show me what I needed to see. I feel, sometimes, as if Melissa was tired, exhausted, of existing for so long, I feel she wanted to end her existence, her undead life. As if, she had given up, allowing me to place that rusty dagger through her cold heart...

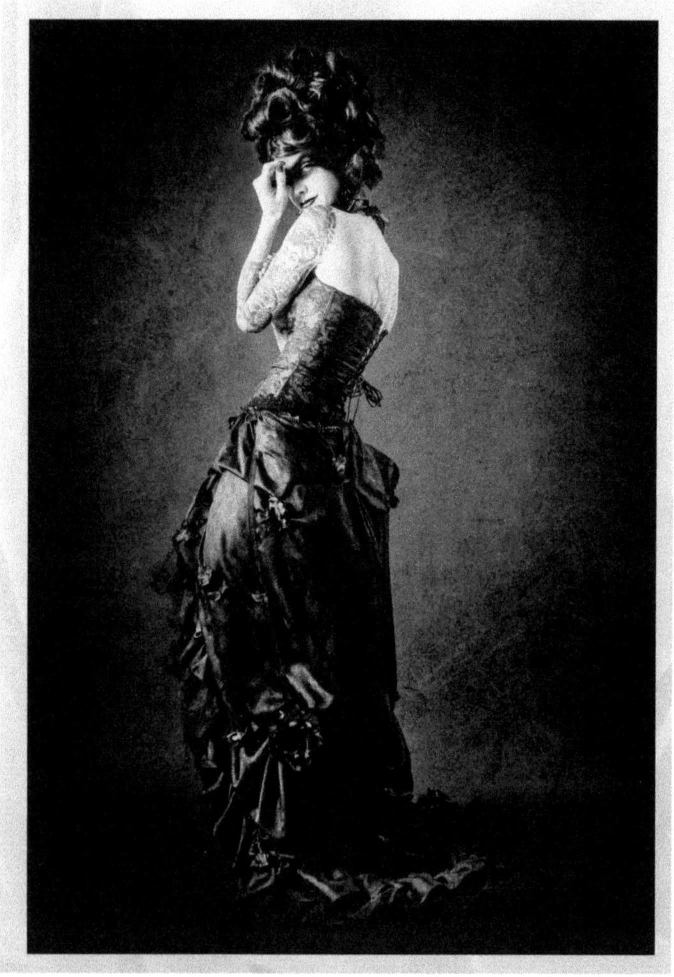

Chapter 10

As all these memories of Melissa swirl in my mind, I reflect back on her ever-loving tales, her stories, she always described to me...

It was one of those rare quiet nights at the brothel house, the kind where the usual ruckus settled into the stillness of shadows and sighs. The air was dry, thick with the scent of candle wax and aged wood, while the distant clinking of glasses from the bar area below was but a murmur. Melissa sat cross-legged on the tussled bed, her raven hair loose, catching the soft, flickering glow of the single candle that barely illuminated the room. Her pale skin glistened like snow amongst the candlelight. Across from her, I leaned in, curiosity dwelling deep within my tired eyes, as Melissa began her story...

"You ever hear about Tristen and Lenore?" Melissa asked, her voice low, a soft whisper, meant only, for these private, darkened hours.

I shook my head, drawing my knees up to my chest, my fingers moving nervously playing with the frayed hem of my gown, "No." I whispered back. "Was it a love story, a tragic one?"

Melissa nodded, a bitter smile curling her lips, "The kind of love story that never should have been, yet it was. They met when the world was young for them, hearts still untouched by the weight of reality. She was a healer's daughter, and he was... well, he was from somewhere far away. A soldier, they would say, though no one was quite sure what he fought for."

"Did he love this, Lenore?" I asked, my voice barely a breath above the candle's faint sputter.

"With all his soul," Melissa replied. "But you know how these stories go. Love, real love, it doesn't come easy, especially when it's too pure for this world."

Melissa's gaze drifted, her mind wandering back to the tale she claimed to have heard so long ago, "They'd meet in secret, just like this, as we are now," she gestured around the dimly lit room. "Under the cover of night, away from prying eyes, speaking of tainted dreams they'd never live to see. Tristen promised Lenore the entire world, it seemed, but she did not want it. She only wanted him, the quieter moments, the stolen kisses in the moonlight."

My breath caught in my throat, as Melissa's tone grew darker, "But Tristen was bound to something deeper than his love for Lenore. There were rumors of a dark curse, whispers of blood debts owed to forces no one dared named. Lenore, in her innocence, thought love could save him from whatever shadows followed him, but love... love isn't always enough."

The candle flickered, casting Melissa's pale face into sharper relief. Her emerald eyes, usually so hard and guarded, softened with the weight of her story, "One night, just before dawn, Tristen didn't come to their meeting place. Lenore waited in the forest, where they always met under the moonlight, under an old maple tree. She waited for several, long hours, her heart growing heavier with each passing moment, until the sun began to rise in the sky. That's when she saw him, or what was left of him."

I gasped, my fingers clutching to the blanket I held, much tighter, I whispered frantically, "What happened, Melissa? You must tell me!"

"He was broken, Maria Grace," Melissa said, her voice barely a whisper now. "Not in body, but in spirit. His eyes were hollow, his skin pale like the dead. He'd been taken by whatever darkness he'd tried so hard to escape. Tristen told her... he told her that they could never be together, not in this life. That whatever was chasing him had caught up to him, and he could not drag her into the abyss with him. He loved her too much to let her fall into death with him."

Tears welled in my eyes, as I faintly asked, "And she believed him?"

Melissa nodded slowly, "What choice did she have? She begged him to stay with her, to fight it, but he was already lost. So, under that old maple tree, where they'd once shared dreams, they said their final goodbye. Tristen kissed her one last time and walked away, disappearing into the mist of the early sunrise. Lenore... she never saw him again."

The room fell completely silent, save for a soft crackling of the candle. I wiped my eyes, my heart aching for a love that was never known, "What happened to her, after that? To Lenore?"

Melissa sighed, leaning back against the headboard, the story still weighing heavily on her, "She waited for him every night after that, every single night, in hopes of his return. Some say she went mad with grief, heartbreak. Others say her heart simply stopped beating when she realized in her older age that he was never coming back. Either way,

Lenore died under that old maple tree, still waiting for the love that had left her behind."

I shivered, the story lingering like a ghost in the room, its sorrow wrapping around me like a cold embrace, "It's so sad," I whispered, "why does love always have to end like this?"

Melissa extinguished the candle that was burning low, with a swift breath, plunging them into complete darkness, "Because, Maria Grace," she said softly, her voice carrying through the blackness, "Real love never leaves, even when it's gone, it stays with you... forever."

Another story surfaced in my mind; one Melissa had told me on those much quieter evenings within the brothel house...

The night was stale, and the brothel house had fallen into its usual state of silence. The heavy velvet curtains were drawn, casting shadows that danced with the flicker of the single candle Melissa held in her hands. She sat on the edge of the bed, her back to the cracked window that let in only the faintest breath of cool air. I was curled up on the wooden floor beside her, cross-legged on a wool blanket, my blue eyes wide, expectant, the exhaustion of the day slowly fading away under the dim light of the room.

"You ever wonder," Melissa began, her voice low, almost swallowed by the stillness, "what happens when you lose someone who feels like a piece of you?"

I looked up at Melissa, my brow furrowed in confusion, "What do you mean?"

Melissa's fingers traced the edge of the candleholder, her emerald eyes distant, as if seeing something far beyond the faded walls of our world, "I knew two women once," she said slowly, letting the words fall like heavy stones, "JoAnna Lynn and Josie Ann. They were... like sisters. Not by blood, but in every other way that mattered. They ran a brothel, much like this one we are in, but theirs, theirs was something else."

I adjusted my position on the blanket, drawing closer, sensing that this tale was going to be different from all the others Melissa had told me me before.

"They started it in a small town on the outskirts of New Orleans," Melissa continued, her voice soft but steady. "This was back in the late 1500's, when women like us didn't have many choices of survival. JoAnna Lynn, she was the older one, strong and tall, with hair as black as midnight and eyes so dark you could swear she saw right through you. Josie Ann, on the other hand, was lighter, in every way. Golden hair that caught the sun, skin like porcelain, and eyes the color of a Spring sky."

"They both sound so beautiful, Melissa." I whispered as I imagined their frames, their appearances.

"They were," Melissa agreed. "But more than that, they were very smart. They knew how to survive in a world that wanted to chew them up and spit them out. They started small, just a room or two for travelers who needed more than a bed for the night, but soon, their place became known. Not just for what you'd expect of it, but for the way they ran things. Their 'hired girls' were treated very well, better than anywhere else. The gentlemen, even the rich ones, knew they had to respect the rules and the girls. It wasn't just a business, it was a sanctuary, a home, for the broken, the lost, and it was all because of those women, JoAnna Lynn and Josie Ann."

Melissa paused, her emerald eyes flickering over to the window where the moonlight struggled to filter through the small gap of the curtains. I watched her closely, sensing the turn in the story, it felt like Melissa was in a deep memory of what could've been her past experiences.

"They weren't just business partners, though," Melissa said softly, "They loved each other, in a way that went beyond what people could understand back then. Not in the romantic sense, but something deeper. They'd grown up together, like siblings, been through the worst of times together. They saved each other, over and over again. When one was down, the other lifted her up. When one was ready to give up on life, the other dragged her through such darkness, never letting each other falter."

My heart ached for these two women that I didn't even know really existed, but already I felt so connected to them, "So, what happened?" I asked, my voice hesitant, as if I feared the answer.

Melissa's gaze darkened, her expression shifting, "Things never stay perfect, Maria Grace. You know that. It was only a matter of time before it all came crashing down."

Melissa shifted on the bed, setting the candle down on the small table beside her, casting long shadows over the room, "It was a man," Melissa said, bitterness coating her words. "It always is. He came into their lives like a storm rages in, charming, wealthy, the kind who knew how to make women feel seen, feel important, confident. His name was Antonio, he was a rich merchant, passing through town on his way to somewhere grander, but he stayed for the love of them, JoAnna Lynn and Josie Ann. At first, he seemed harmless, someone just looking for a good time. But he had an eye for Josie Ann, and soon enough, she started falling for him."

My heart dropped, already knowing where this story was heading.

"JoAnna Lynn didn't fully trust him from the start," Melissa said, shaking her head. "She'd seen men like him before, men who were used to getting what they wanted, no matter who they had to destroy to get it. She warned Josie Ann, but love makes you blind, or at least, it makes you ignore the things you do not want to truly see."

I could feel the tension in the room, the heaviness of the tale settling like a weight on my chest.

"Antonio started driving the two women apart, slowly at first, in ways you wouldn't notice right away. He'd tell Josie Ann that she deserved more, that she was a better woman than running a place like this. He made her feel like the life her and JoAnna Lynn had built wasn't enough for her anymore, and she actually started to believe his words. She stopped working as much, spending all her time with Antonio, dreaming of a different life that was never going to be, while JoAnna Lynn carried the burden of running the brothel alone."

Melissa's voice grew quieter, but more intense, like she was reliving the pain of the story herself, "JoAnna Lynn tried to hold it all together, tried to remind Josie Ann of what they had created together, of all they had built, but it was too late. Antonio had his sharp claws in too deep, and one night, it all came to a head. They argued, JoAnna Lynn and Josie Ann, worse than they ever had before. Words were said that could never be taken back."

Melissa's hands clenched into fists, her pale knuckles becoming whiter, "JoAnna Lynn told Josie Ann that if she walked out the door of the brothel with Antonio, there'd be no coming back. That'd she would lose everything, including her, but Josie Ann... she left anyway."

Tears forming in the corners of my blue eyes, "Did she ever come back?"

Melissa shook her head slowly, "No. She didn't. JoAnna Lynn never saw her again. Word spread through the town, whispers, that Josie Ann and Antonio had ran off together, left town, but... it wasn't the happy ending she thought it would be. Antonio drained her of what little wealth she had with her, used her until she was left to nothing, and when he was done, he left her in a place far worse than where she had started. Josie Ann died penniless and broken, heartbroken, alone, a shadow of the woman she used to be."

I gasped a short breath, my heart breaking for that woman who had lost everything, "And JoAnna Lynn, what became of her?" I asked, my voice barely able to utter the words.

Melissa's face was unreadable, her expression tight with much sorrow of the story, "JoAnna Lynn stayed in that brothel, alone. She kept it running, but it wasn't the same without her companion, Josie Ann. Her heart, her unrelated sister, was gone. She never really forgave herself for letting Josie Ann leave, and, in a way, she never forgave her for actually leaving. Some say JoAnna Lynn aged gracefully, dying in her lonely bed, but with a broken heart, while others say she just disappeared one night, walking into the bayou, never to be seen again."

The room fell into a heavy silence, the only faint sound was the light crackle of the candle. I wiped a tear from my cheek, feeling the emotion of the tragic tale settle deep into my bones, "Why do all the good things, the good relationships, have to end in such tragedy?" I asked, my voice trembling.

Melissa looked at me, her eyes dark and lost within the candlelight, "Because, Maria Grace, the world wasn't made for love and friendship like that to exist, it wasn't made for women like us."

I reflect back on another romantic, tragedy that Melissa once told me, an immortal tale...

'In the shadowy alleyways of Seville, where the cobblestones glistened under the pale moonlight, Elena found solace from her mundane life. As the daughter of a humble merchant, her days were spent amidst the bustling markets, but her heart longed for something more. She often dreamed of passion, adventure, and the kind of love that stories were spun from, one that would sweep her off her feet and transport her world far removed from her own. One late evening, drawn by the sweet strumming of a frail guitar, Elena wandered into a secluded courtyard. It was here she first saw him, a figure of a man cloaked in darkness, his eyes gleaming like twin stars against the night. He was unlike anyone she had ever encountered: tall with jet-black hair that cascaded like a waterfall over his shoulders, and a presence that felt both magnetic and foreboding, almost hypnotizing. His name was Damian, a name she would come to remember with both longing and sorrow. Their eyes met, and in that instant, the world around them faded into a distant echo. Elena felt an overwhelming pull toward him, as if the very fabric of fate had woven their destinies together. Damian, a vampire cursed to wander the earth alone, found in Elena an ancient warmth that thawed the ice encasing his undead, cold heart. As nights, turned into weeks, their clandestine meetings grew bolder, hidden from the prying eyes of a society that would never accept their love. Under the moonlight, they would dance in the privacy of the courtyard, surrounded by shadows that twirled with them from the candlelight. Damian taught her his world, tales of ancient castles and forgotten love, of battles fought and lost, and of the darkness that enveloped his never dying soul. Elena listened, enthralled, her heart racing, mesmerized, with each whispered secret. She saw in his hollow eyes a deep loneliness that resonated with her own unfulfilled dreams. Yet, beneath the enchanting allure of their intimate romance lay a bitter truth. Elena was mortal, a human, a fleeting spark in the eternal darkness of Damian's existence. As their love deepened, Elena felt the weight of time pressing upon her like a looming specter. She would age while Damian remained forever young, her vitality waning as he stood untouched by the passage of years.

The fateful night finally arrived, drenched in an oppressive silence. Elena, burdened by the inevitability of their separation, found herself at the courtyard once more. Damian stood there, the moonlight casting long shadows across his face, revealing the pain etched into his masculine, seductive features. He reached for her hand, and she could feel the coldness of his touch seep through her skin, stirring both fear and longing within her. "Elena," he began, his voice a deep, haunting melody, "the darkness that surrounds me is relentless. I want to offer you eternity, an eternity with me, but it would mean sacrificing your very soul. I cannot bear the thought of your light fading away in my shadow."

Tears glistened in Elena's eyes as she stepped closer, her heart aching, "But I would rather fade away with you than live a lifetime without you, without your love. You are my light, my salvation, Damian."

He shook his head, anguish spilling from his eyes, "No, my love. You do not know what you ask of me. Your light must shine bright in this darkened world. You deserve a life filled with much laughter and warmth, not one entwined with mere darkness."

As the moon rose high in the sky, illuminating their tragic dilemma, Elena felt her heart shatter, "I cannot lose you, Damian. I would follow you into the depths of hell if it meant I could be with you."

Damian's expression turned grave. "You must choose Elena. If you stay, you will become a part of the darkness, doing things you've never experienced, like drinking the blood of a mortal and never seeing the sunlight again. The beautiful human that you are, will become dark, and your sweet laughter will fade, your dreams will wither, and you will remain for all eternity. Eternity is a very long time to dwell on this earth, especially if you are alone."

The choice hung heavy between them, an unbearable weight that threatened to crush Elena's spirit, and yet, in her heart, she knew the truth, she knew that Damian was right, that his words were truth. As the dawn threatened to break, casting shadows that danced away, she whispered, "I cannot do this to you, I cannot do something that will make you stop loving me. I will not become a shadow of your sorrow, Damian. I only wanted to be with you forever."

With that, Elena turned to leave, her heart breaking with every step. Damian watched her go, his heart shattering, saddened, as the distance between them grew. The light of dawn began to creep into the courtyard, a bittersweet reminder of the life that awaited her beyond the horizon, a life that Damian could never be a part of. Days turned into months, and Elena felt the life within her slowly begin to fade, 'had she made the right choice?' The joy that once filled her heart was replaced by a hollow ache, a void, the memory of Damian haunting her dreams. As the sun set each night, she would stand in the same courtyard, waiting for a glimpse of the man, the vampire, who had ignited her soul, but he never came. He was bound by his immortal curse, unable to cross the threshold of the dawn that heralded her freedom, and so, she faded, an ethereal whisper in the wind, a memory trapped in the shadows. The last of Elena's strength slipped away as she stood beneath the moon, her heart forever tethered to Damian's. With each passing moment, she felt herself drifting further from the world, her heartache never ceasing, like mist on a summer morning. In her final breath, she whispered his name, a promise carried into the night.

Damian, lost in the depths of his immortal sorrow, remained in the courtyard long after Elena's light had vanished. He never thought she would end it all so quickly, he had hoped she would find happiness beyond him, in her mortal life. The moon cast its silvery glow on his pale face, but the warmth of their love was now a distant memory. For all eternity, he would walk the earth alone, bound by the darkness that had claimed his undead heart. As the sun rose, its light banishing the shadows, Damian knew he would forever mourn the woman who had dared to love him as the evil creature he was. In the stillness of the dawn, he vowed to always remember her, a ray of light in his endless night. Damian disappeared into the darkness, never to love again.'

Reflecting back on these saddened tales, I can't help but feel that Melissa was telling me her true story through these made-up myths. My undead heart ached for her lost soul, wherever it may dwell now...

Chapter 11

As I stand, remaining on the edge of eternity, I find myself intertwined with the very fabric of my city, New Orleans, a city that has witnessed countless tales of love, loss, and redemption. My journey, a tapestry woven with threads of light and shadow, leads me to better understand that immortality is not merely a gift, but a curse, a burden laden with the weight of memories.

Reflecting on my estranged life as Maria Grace, a name I hold proudly now, I am both the young girl who once believed in the sweetness of love and the woman, the vampire, who now walks the night, carrying the eternal scars of betrayal and many regrets. Each soul, each life, I've encountered, each life I've touched, each one I have taken, has become a part of me, echoing in the stillness of my undead heart. I have loved fiercely, lost profoundly, and ultimately learned that the essence of existence is found not just in moments of joy, but in sad lessons etched with much sorrow.

Melissa, with her haunting beauty and her untold past, remains a bittersweet memory, a reminder of the complexities of such love and hard sacrifices. The night I ended her existence is forever etched in my mind, a culmination of much pain that transformed me into the very creature I now embody. In her death, I lost a part of myself, yet I gained the clarity of the truth, a clarity to forge my own eternal path, one that acknowledges the darkness while embracing the light.

As I continue to wander through these vibrant streets of this city, this French Quarter, the echoes of all its history over the many centuries, resonate deep within me. Each sunset paints the sky with the dark colors of countless stories, a reminder that mortal life is fleeting, yet eternal life is unbearable at times in its full essence. I am a keeper of these age-old stories, a guardian of the memories that linger like whispers in the wind, never before told, until now, but before I finish my story, I would like to leave you with one last tale that Melissa had once told me...

'In the heart of Spain... on a humid summer evening in the heart of Seville, Spain, Mateo, a rugged but gentle artist with dreams of creating something meaningful, stands in the dim glow of lanterns in the plaza, sketching the lines of the historic architecture. On the opposite end of the square, a young woman, Isabel, is silently absorbing the beauty of the plaza that is all around her. She is a free spirit, intelligent, and ambitious, though bound by her family's rigid expectations. Her life has been mapped out by her family, who is deeply entrenched in the world of politics. They meet by pure chance when Isabel accidentally bumps into Mateo, causing his sketchbook to fall to the dusty ground. He recognizes her from her sketches, as he's watched her from afar in the square on multiple occasions. Their conversation is short yet charged with a tension that is both thrilling and intimidating. The connection is instantaneous, both feeling a sense of recognition, as if they'd known each other before, like in another life. That night, they part ways, but neither of them can shake the feeling that fate had drawn them together. Little do they know, but their paths would cross again, though not under the same circumstances they might've hoped for. Mateo and Isabel encounter each other in the days that follow, each meeting marked by a growing intensity and undeniable attraction. They begin sharing stories, Isabel sharing about her family's influence over her future and Mateo about his struggle as an artist trying to survive in a city that often dismisses dreams. She's drawn to his intense passion and honesty, a stark contrast to the cold, calculated world she has been raised in. Mateo, meanwhile, sees Isabel as his muse, a woman who embodies the beauty and tragedy of the city itself. One night, beneath the sprawling olive trees, they share their very first kiss. It's both a promise and a curse. Isabel confesses her fears of disappointing her family, and Mateo listens, understanding that their worlds are incompatible. He knows that pursuing Isabel would mean going against everything she's been taught to value. Despite this, they cannot resist meeting, sneaking through the quiet alleyways and hidden gardens. As the days turn to weeks, they become enraptured in a whirlwind romance, meeting in secret to escape the demands and expectations of their separate lives, but as their love grows, so does the realization that they are on borrowed time. Isabel's family becomes suspicious, particularly her oldest brother, Javier, who holds ambitions of his own and has noticed her strange absences. He confronts Isabel one late evening, urging her to consider their family's reputation and the political alliance they're trying to forge with another influential family. Isabel's heart sinks as she learns about her parents' plans to marry her off to Alejandro, a man of wealth and great power. The weight of her family's demands feels unbearable, but she finds a fragile solace in her secret affair, her forbidden meetings with Mateo. However, Mateo grows restless, sensing the impending shadow of their separation. He urges her to just leave her family, to live for herself, but Isabel knows the cost of such rebellion. It would mean abandoning not just her family but her entire world and putting both her life and Mateo's at risk. Caught between loyalty and love, Isabel becomes increasingly tormented. Her family's plans for her become more pressing, yet she cannot bring herself to abandon Mateo. Their passion becomes an aching, destructive force, as their love is painted with the pain of what they can never fully have. Isabel reaches a breaking point. Her family announces her immediate engagement to Alejandro at a grand celebration within the square, making her realize the permanence of her predicament. In a desperate moment, she sneaks away to find Mateo, trembling with the knowledge of what this engagement really means. They embrace under the glowing moonlight, whispering false promises and curses against fate. Mateo, desperate to hold onto Isabel, pleads with her to just run away with him. He envisions a better life in the countryside, away from society's gaze, where they can live simply, far from the shadows of expectation and obligation. But, Isabel, bound by her inner fears, tells him she can't just leave her family. The thought of living in exile, of becoming an outcast, is one she cannot bring herself to accept. A rift forms between them as they both realize that the forbidden dreams, they hold for their lives may not be compatible. In one final embrace, Mateo and Isabel cling to each other with such passion, each knowing that it might be their last embrace. As the dawn breaks, Isabel returns to her family, sealing her fate to Alejandro. Haunted by their separation, Mateo begins to unravel, his heartbreak is almost unbearable. His art, once a source of solace, becomes dark and very twisted, reflecting his anguish. Isabel's absence leaves him in a state of despair, unable to envision a future without her. Meanwhile, Isabel endures her dreaded engagement preparations, hiding her broken heart under a facade of obedience. Though she tries to forget Mateo, her soul remains tethered to him. Driven by much heartache, Mateo makes one last attempt to see Isabel, risking everything. He confronts her at a secluded garden where they had once met, demanding to know if she ever loved him or if it was all a fleeting passion for her. Isabel, conflicted and filled with guilt, admits that her heart belongs to him but insists they can never have any type of future together. With those words, Mateo feels himself shatter. He leaves her, each step pulling him further from the only happiness he's ever truly known. Time passes, but neither Mateo nor Isabel, can truly let it all go. Mateo descends deeper into despair, neglecting his art and becoming a ghost of the man, he once was. Isabel, meanwhile, moves forward, sadly, with her marriage to Alejandro, feeling as though she's walking into a gilded prison. She's constantly reminded of the life she could've had, and the love she abandoned. In a final act of mere desperation, Mateo sends Isabel a letter, telling her that he's leaving Seville for good, hoping to find peace elsewhere. The letter shakes Isabel to her very core, reigniting her hidden love for him and making her question everything. She wrestles with the forbidden idea of meeting Mateo one last time, torn between duty and her inner desire. On a stormy night in Seville, Isabel sneaks out to see Mateo. They meet by the river, where they shared so many false dreams. It's there that they make a final, heartbreaking decision. Unable to live without each other but unwilling to defy the lives they are bound to, they share one last kiss and vow that if fate doesn't allow them to ever be together in this present life, then perhaps in the next life to come. Months after their final encounter together, Mateo is found dead in his small , dim room, surrounded by his unfinished sketches, his unfinished paintings of Isabel. He had left one last painting of her by the river, their final meeting immortalized in brush strokes. His death is ruled as a suicide, though many suspect he simply died of a broken heart. When the tragic news reached Isabel, she's inconsolable, though she is forced to maintain her outward composure. The memories of her love, her Mateo, haunt her daily, each place they once walked together now a painful reminder of the love she sacrificed. Though she remains married to Alejandro, her spirit grows weaker with each passing year, as though part of her had died along with Mateo. Isabel grew old, yet remained heartbroken, eventually dying in her sleep. In the many years that followed, locals would speak of a haunting in the old plaza where Mateo and Isabel first met, rumors of a woman and a man seen embracing under the dim, lantern light. Some would say it's the spirits of a couple torn apart yet reunited at last. Though it's dismissed as a story to entertain through the ages, those who actually knew them will always remember, forever haunted by the love that defied time but was shattered by the weight of their own bitter choices.'

In the end, my reflections reveal that to be immortal, a vampire, is to be forever entwined with the human experience, an immortal witness to the beautiful tragedy of mere existence. Love, in all its many forms, remains the greatest mystery of all, and the deepest wound. It binds us, heals us, and in its absence, leaves us yearning for connection in a world often shrouded in shadows.

So here I stand, Maria Grace, forever a vampire, forever a seeker of more understanding, navigating the complexities of this immortal life. As I embrace the echoes of my past, trying to always hold on to the memories, I step into the future with an open, undead heart, ready to face, to embrace, the love that faintly lingers, the hopes that dimly still flicker, and the stories that have yet to be written, to be told.

This is my reflection, a journey through darkness and light, a testament to the resilience of the human spirit, even when it wears the guise of the undead, and as I pen these final words to paper, I invite you to walk with me, to share with me, in the whispers of a life that transcends time and embraces the eternal dance of love and great loss.

So, this is my story, my tale... I still keep the old, silver vintage mirror close to me, looking at it very often, to remind myself who I really am, who Melissa really was, a vampire. My reflection is pale white, as I look at my glassy white skin with the same ravenous, black hair and eyes of deep blue, the same as before during my mortal days. Yet, my skin is much paler now than in my human years. I still reside in the French Quarter of New Orleans, where I will always remain, within the old brothel house, which is now my renovated hotel. I will forever hold Melissa, my savior, my protector, my means of an immortal existence, in my thoughts and within my undying heart...

Reflections of a Vampire, my memoir, is now told.

Poem: Vampire in the Mirror

The Vampire in the Mirror

In the quiet of night, where the moon hangs low,
A shadow moves where no winds blow,
She stands alone, her heart long still,
Bound to darkness, against her will.

Her eyes, like ice, hold stories untold,
Of centuries lived, of love grown cold,
With pale hands she grasps the frame,
Of a mirror that whispers her fragile name.

The Vampire in the Mirror stares back at me,
A ghostly reflection that none else can see,
No heartbeat, no breath, just a hollowed soul,
A creature cursed to pay immortality's toll.

Once, I was human, fragile and small,
With dreams that stretched beyond these walls,
Now I dwell in the night's cold embrace,
An echo of life, with no saving grace.

I remember the time I first felt the change,
When a Vampire came, mysterious and strange,
She healed my sickness, my body revived,
But the price was my mother, no longer alive.

I wept by her side as the life drained away,
And the Vampire stood, cold, with nothing to say,
Her eyes gleamed bright, her lips tasted red,
While my mother's blood was all that she fed.

Years passed in a haze of forgotten despair,
Till love bloomed in secret, a fragile affair,
My lover, my light in a world of pain,
Yet even that joy could not remain.

For the Vampire, possessive, and full of desire,
Took him away, consumed in her fire,
I was left with only the silence and tears,
Haunted by shadows, consumed by fears.

Then came the night when I took my stand,
With a dagger of iron in my trembling hand,
The Vampire's betrayal had cut far too deep,
And the demon inside her I no longer could keep.

With fury, I struck, and she bit back hard,
Our lives intertwined, forever scarred,
As her blood stained my lips, I fell to the floor,
The child I was, existed no more.

Now I rise, each night, under starlit skies,
With memories of sorrow, clouding my eyes,
The Vampire in the Mirror, with lips of red,
Is all that's left of the life I once led.

No pulse beneath my skin, no warmth to feel,
A hunger that gnaws, a wound that won't heal,
I search for my soul in that silvered glass,
A reflection trapped in the moments that pass.

She watches me, the creature I've become,
With whispers of love, but I've grown numb,
For the Vampire in the Mirror, though she wears my face,
Is no longer tied to time or place.

I chase after dreams that I can't relive,
But the shadows only take, they never give,
A century's love, a lifetime of blood tears,
Swallowed by decades, erased by years.

Still, I hold the Mirror close to my chest,
A relic of grief, a token of rest,
It shows me the truth that I cannot flee,
That the Vampire in the Mirror will always be me.

So I wander the nights, adrift, alone,
In a world where stars have hearts of stone,
The Vampire in the Mirror, her gaze so clear,
Is the only reflection I will ever fear.

Poem: A Twisted Oak

A Twisted Oak

Beneath the moon's cold, silver stare,
A twisted Oak stands, roots laid bare,
Its branches reach like fingers torn,
From earth's deep womb, dark secrets born,
Its bark is black, like sins confessed,
A graveyard's breath upon its crest,
Once proud, once tall, now bent and scarred,
A witness to two hearts, love-marred,
They met beneath its shadowed veil,
A tale of love, now sharp as nails,
His eyes like night, her hair like flame,

But fate's cruel hand would play its game,
Beneath this tree, where whispers bleed,
They swore their love, and hearts would heed,
But blood was spilt, and vows were torn,
Their love turned ghost, forever mourned,
Now twisted wood and hollow cries,
Mingle with the midnight skies,
A tree of sorrow, dark and grim,
Where lovers' souls twist limb to limb,
So if you pass, be sure to flee,
From the shadow of the oak tree,
For it still hungers, still it waits,
To bind another to its fate.

Poem: Reflections in Silver

Reflections in Silver

In velvet dark, where shadows creep,
I find the place where none dare sleep.
Ans in my hand, a mirror cold,
Silver and small, yet centuries old.

Its frame is etched with time's cruel art,
Each line, a mark upon my heart,
I gaze into its glassy face,
And see what time cannot erase.

My reflection stares, eternally young,
Yet silent songs my soul has sung,
No breath to fog the silver gleam,
No pulse to quicken, no waking dream.

But once... oh, once, when I was she,
A mortal child of earth and sea,
I knew the warmth of summer's kiss,
I lived within the light I miss.

I held this mirror, just a girl,
And twirled beneath the world's soft swirl,
The sky was vast, the wind was kind,
And in that glass, I knew my mind.

But the nights grew long, the shadows fell,
And in their arms, I tasted Hell,
The darkness called, a voice so sweet,
I followed blindly, incomplete.

A stranger's smile, a stranger's bite,
And thus began my endless night,
Now time, for me, a hollow thing,
A wheel that turns without a spring.

I hold the mirror close once more,
A relic from the life before,
And in its glass, a face I see,
But it is not what once was me.

The girl who laughed, who danced, who dreamed,
Now lost within this cursed gleam,
Her skin was flushed, her eyes alive,
But now I watch her fade, deprived.

The mirror knows, the mirror sees,
The mortal joy, the simple ease,
Of breathing air, of tasting wine,
Of feeling hunger's mortal sign.

I ache for days of fleeting sun,
For time that ends, a race once run,
To age, to wither, to decay,
But all of that was stripped away.

My beauty lingers, cold as frost,
An ageless curse, a grievous cost,
The mirror shows me what I've gained,
But never speaks of what remains.

I touch the glass, no warmth returns,
No flicker of the life that burns,
Instead, I see the hollow stare,
Of something more than death's despair.

Undying, yes, but not alive,
A ghost who never can arrive,
At my end, at any peace.
For time itself will never cease.

In this reflection, I am bound,
A silent scream without a sound,
The girl I was, forever gone,
But I am left to carry on.

A vampire's curse, a mirror's gleam,
A hollow life, a broken dream,
I hold the glass, my endless friend,
And wonder when this night will end.

For though I live, I do not thrive,
I'm trapped inside this deathless lie,
This mirror shows me all I lack,
A face of beauty, staring back.

But beauty fades in light of truth,
And I have lost my endless youth,
Though time cannot my face erase,
It steals my heart in its embrace.

So now I stand, forever here,
No breath to sigh, no tear to tear,
Just me, this mirror, and the night,
Reflected in its silver light.

And as I gaze, I see her still,
That girl, once bright, whose heart could feel,
But now her memory slowly dies,
Behind these cold, immortal eyes.

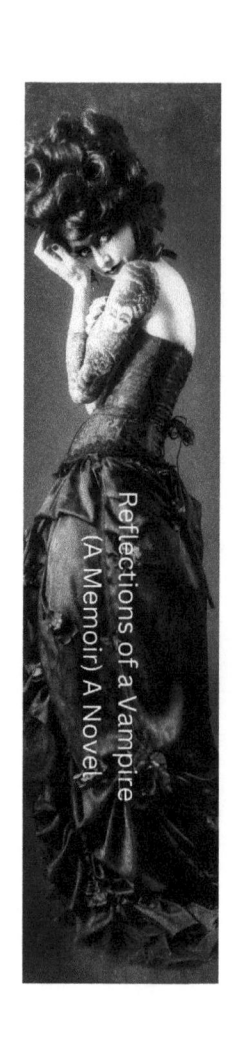

Reflections of a Vampire (A Memoir) A Novel

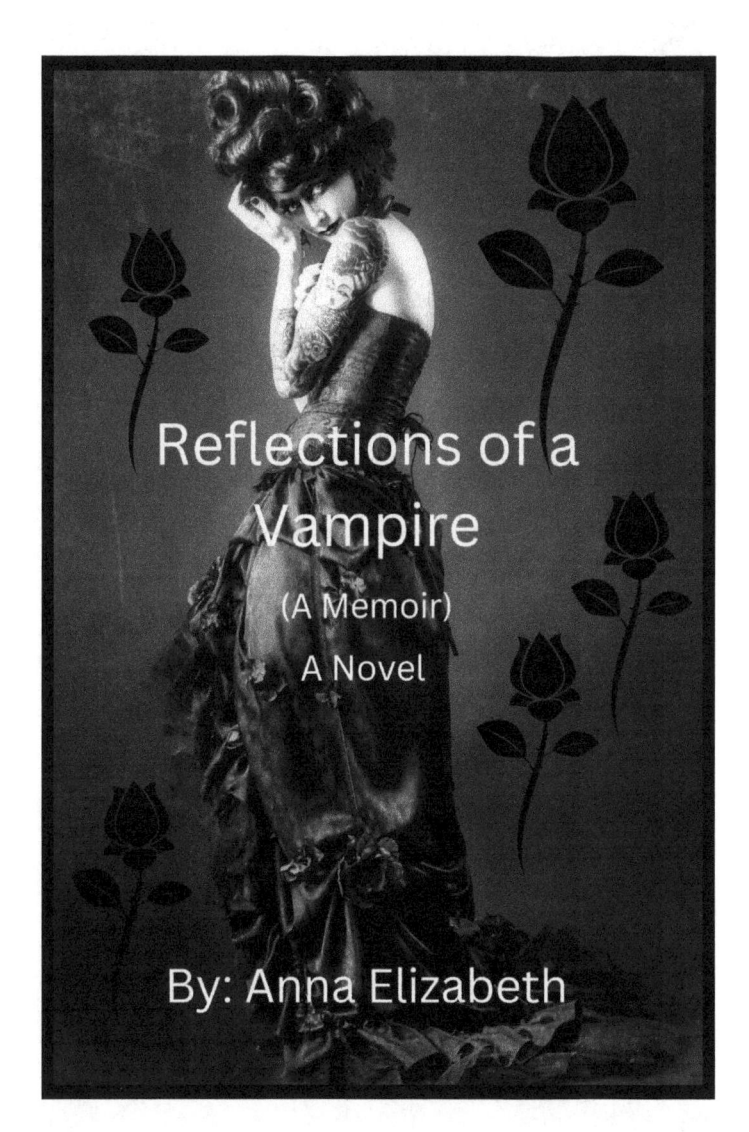

Reflections of a Vampire

(A Memoir)

A Novel

By: Anna Elizabeth

Looking back. Reflections of one's life.
The pain, the sadness, only moments of bitter happiness.
So, my tale can now be told.
I'm Maria Grace.
An immortal.
This story is not for the faint of heart. It was my life as a mortal until I was turned.
Secrets untold, now revealed.
The past to the present, a life of regrets, and choices made.
Take this journey into my dark world, you'll never again be the same.

Reflections of a Vampire

Reflections of a Vampire
(A Memoir)
A Novel
By: Anna Elizabeth

Reflections of a Vampire